RISING SUN

New Seattle Book Two

M.J. O'SHEA

Rising Sun M.J. O'Shea

Published by MJ O'Shea https://www.mjoshea.com

Printed in The United States

Cover Artist: M.J. O'Shea

Chapter One

New Seattle 2199

*THESE PEOPLE HAVE no idea what easy targets they are...
all it takes is a simple flick of the wrist, and they're mine. All
of them.*

Jaffa Sharp slinked through the teeming market in
Metrolevel, the center of New Seattle.

It wasn't as cushy as the market up top supposedly was,
the one on Cloud Level, where only the best merchants and
most exclusive customers were allowed, nor was it seedy
like some of the stalls down in the lower levels of New
Seattle.

Down below, Jaffa could probably find all sorts of less
than legal things, including a knife or two in his gut. He
mostly stayed away from the lower levels. He ran fast but
not that fast and he considered his entrails his best friends.
He had no interest in being parted from them.

Metrolevel Market was crowded and bright, mostly safe
and full of people. Rich, fat merchants, complacent and
bossy, swathed in lush fabrics and layers of belts barely able

to hold in their prodigious paunches. Squeezed between the stalls flowed hordes of chattering women and unruly children, who dodged their mamas distracted grasps.

They were all like sheep, these people, oblivious to anything but their own busy, shallow lives and practically waiting to be swiftly and silently divested of their fleece.

Jaffa was more than happy to lighten their load.

The market's stall owners were a bit more wary. Jaffa had to be careful of them. Sometimes he could filch a few plump simu-fruits from one or perhaps a small laser blade or trinket from another to sell later, but never anything too big.

Any large-scale thieving attempt from the stall owners would be stupidity itself, enough to land him on a hard-labor crew or exiled somewhere in sweaty stinking Bottom City.

He was smarter than that.

Besides, Jaffa had no need to steal large items, when purses and hip pouches were so easily slit open and drained of their contents. Coins and cards were his before the owner even knew they'd been taken.

Yes. No point in stealing too much from the stalls. He could *buy* anything he wanted once the rich people's unwatched money was his.

Metrolevel Market was uncharacteristically steamy that day, still lit from within by the artificial lights that held the outside's permanent darkness at bay, but hot and sticky. Unpleasant. Nothing like the usual, perfect level of engineered comfort. Jaffa noticed merchants fanning themselves, women unwinding layers of bright scarves.

Perhaps some cheeky prankster had tampered with the atmospheric controllers, he decided. There weren't many other possibilities. The interior of the city cooled and warmed gradually by the month, mirroring the old seasons to give inhabitants an illusion of the climate changes of the past, but it had never been either hot or cold before. Not in his lifetime.

Jaffa realized he had actually broken out in a sweat, something that usually only happened if he ventured down below, where the monstrous, yawning turbines pumped exhaust from all of Seattle into Bottom City, the only level that remained unwalled, uncontrolled, and naturally dark.

Things in Metrolevel didn't feel quite right.

No matter, though. He had work to do. Jaffa brushed off the nagging unease and concentrated on his task. It was life or death. Literally. He'd have no food to eat if his fingers weren't nimble enough to steal, and the thought of getting caught... well, it was unthinkable. Market day was no time to be distracted.

Unlike the watchful stall owners, merchants were often careless. They made the best targets—too puffed full of their own self-importance, and quite a bit more food than Jaffa ever saw, to notice the world around them. Busy, harried upper-class servants were easy to divest of goods as well, although he hesitated to steal from them. Even Jaffa had morals, and he hated to get someone in trouble who worked hard for their wages.

On rare occasions, the upper echelons themselves sometimes descended from Cloud Level to experience the busiest market in New Seattle. Doe-eyed and overwhelmed by all the sights and sounds, they tripped around in their expensive diaphanous silks with more money than Jaffa could even comprehend dangling from their wrists in thin fabric purses.

They were a temptation, and most likely the easiest targets of them all, but the possible consequences of stealing from a high-born Dragon or a Phoenix, or even a lesser Scorpion or Griffin or Cobra, weren't worth even the vast wealth they carried. Jaffa liked his head connected to his body and would prefer it stayed that way, thanks.

Getting caught stealing from one of the triads was a sure way to lose it.

Jaffa wove his way through the market, slitting purses and pockets, collecting enough to buy food for the week. He had to use the cards before anyone noticed they were gone, so he could only take a few at a time. It was best not to be greedy. Greed was what got people like him caught.

Up ahead he saw a young man, probably only a few years older than his own twenty, maybe not even that. He had a shock of bright orange hair, nearly Kovalenko Dragon red but not quite dark and rich enough to look like one of the snooty lords of the land. Still, he was visibly expensive, from Upper Metro at least, gesturing and talking a mile a minute to the girl he was with.

He was loud. Distracted. An easy target.

Those kinds of people usually had enough funds on them to feed him for weeks, and even if he happened to be Dragon adjacent, Jaffa doubted he was anyone of importance. He hoped. Jaffa got ready for the strike.

Duck behind the stall, hide in the crowd, slide in between the target and the person behind him and—

"Ow! What the hell?"

Damn. Damn, damn, fucking damn.

He was caught.

CASTOR KOVALENKO KNEW when he was about to get robbed, and that telltale tug, indiscernible to most but not somebody who'd done all the things he'd done, told him to turn and grab as fast and as hard as he could, or he'd be divested of the contents of his entire bag, legal and, well, not so legal. He couldn't afford to lose either one.

In his grasp he found a bedraggled little ragamuffin with unevenly chopped brown-gold hair, pale unmanicured skin, and luminous blue eyes far too huge for his tiny thin face. It was just a boy. For a moment Castor felt bad, but then he remembered he'd been about to lose a lot of money to this one little boy. His empathy hardened.

"Do you know what happens to people who steal from Dragons?"

He let his voice slip into a whisper, and while most knew Castor as a fun-loving party prince, he had his dangerous side. He'd been trained as an assassin for his uncle, Yuri Kovalenko, one of the triad leaders of the city. He might look like an irresponsible, highborn fool, but there was quite a bit more than that under his surface.

"Pretty sure it doesn't involve me keeping all my parts." The boy's voice was deeper than Castor expected. It didn't match his doe eyes and delicate body.

"C'mon, kid. I've gotta bring you in. I'll tell them you didn't take anything. They'll probably just put you in lockup for the night." Castor got a querulous look for his efforts.

"I ain't a kid."

"Fine. Not a kid. You might want to get rid of anything else you took. Even my good word won't help you much if you have some rich lady's cards hidden on you."

Castor took not-a-kid by the scruffy collar of his tunic and led him toward the market's security station.

It was hypocritical, and he felt a bit bad about the whole thing, but he couldn't ask the city officials to turn a blind eye to his and his brother's own less-than-legal activities if he didn't throw them a bone once in a while. This raggedy little pickpocket was a juicy enough bone to keep them off his case for at least a month.

"What's your name?" The boy glared at him sullenly, and Castor rolled his eyes. "I'm not going to hurt you."

"But you are going to turn me into the police. Why should I tell you anything?"

"No matter. They'll scan your chip anyway." Castor shrugged. He didn't have time for word games. He'd let the officials deal with it. "It won't take more than a second for them to find out who you are."

The boy looked at Castor incredulously. "You think they bother to chip underbelly scum like me? I was born in the streets, not in some cushy Metrolevel hospital like you."

Metrolevel? Pfft. Apparently, he'd been underestimated. Also apparent was that not-a-kid didn't get out much if he didn't recognize Castor's face.

Of course, they didn't chip people like Castor either, but for the opposite reason. Triad families were free to do as they pleased, without the constant surveillance the rest of the city's tax-paying inhabitants were subjected to.

Castor didn't push the angry boy any more. He simply held on to a scrawny little wrist and wove his way through the crowd, used to blending in despite his quasi-highborn status.

In truth, he was simply a Dragon cousin, not a son. Nobody cared about the cousins, and Castor worked that to his advantage constantly. He had money and enough status to get him what he wanted, but not enough to hinder him. Typical bitching aside, as far as he was concerned, his situation was pretty much perfect.

About a hundred feet away from the security stand, Castor felt a rough jerk on his hand. He turned only to find his little captive quickly blending into the crowd.

"Stop!" He tried to chase him for a good fifty feet, but it was no use. The boy was gone, small and quick, an expert in disappearing.

Castor swore under his breath. There went his peace offering. He'd have to find another. No matter. Castor had other things on his mind.

Lynx...

His cousin Lynx had been gone for six days with no word. Six days. Castor wasn't worried. He was terrified. Lynx, as a Dragon son, even though he was second born and not first, never went unaccounted for for more than a few hours. Overnight at best.

Never for days.

Castor was sure there was something wrong. He hadn't shown up for training with Castor and his twin Pollux, he hadn't been at dinner or breakfast or lunch. His room was un-entered and empty. Castor's aunt and uncle had told everyone Lynx was on a trip. They seemed unconcerned. Castor's cousin Leo, heir to the Dragon throne, was equally unconcerned. Castor wasn't fooled.

Something was wrong with the whole situation. Very wrong. Every instinct he had told him that Lynx wasn't on vacation, off on an island pleasure cruiser somewhere. He'd been acting strange even before he'd disappeared. Castor and his brother Pollux were determined to find him.

"OH, BROTHER MINE, I HAVE RETURNED." Castor sailed into the quiet of their cloud-level loft.

It was silent, for once, no after-party friends sprawled drunkenly on the furniture, no customers, no haze of smoke from whatever drug Pollux or he was sampling with potential buyers. Peace. Serenity. Only the well-mannered hiss of the doors sliding to a close behind him. To be honest, it was a little unnerving.

The door to Pollux's room opened, and he came wandering out, scrubbing a hand through his bright shock of red hair, sleep pants slung low across lean muscled hips. "Why you gotta be so loud, bro? I was trying to sleep off last night. When did you leave this morning anyway?"

"Early." Castor shrugged.

Unlike his brother, he didn't require much sleep, so he was accustomed to making their market runs, trading for sellable drugs and party favors in the relative shelter of the teeming middle-class Metrolevel Market.

He never went to the bottom alone, or even the lower levels of midtown. Then he brought his brother. Pollux was no larger or better trained for danger than he, but in dangerous situations, there was always comfort in numbers.

"Any luck?" Pollux scratched at his belly.

"I sold all the bump. Nearly got pick pocketed." He rolled his eyes.

Even though the brat hadn't been successful, it still annoyed Castor that he'd gotten as close as he had. Nobody pulled the slip on him or his brother. Getting stolen from was for the pampered princes and princesses who never left their rarified cloud-level compounds, not for people like him and his brother.

Pollux chuckled. "I'm sure that was the highlight of your morning. Did you turn him in?"

"Bastard got away." He hated admitting that to his brother. They prided themselves on a good record. Losing a thief to the market crowd wasn't a shining moment.

Pollux snickered.

"Fuck off. He was a slippery little sucker. Have you heard any word from Lynx?"

They weren't as close to their cousin as they'd been when they were children, but typically if he was going to be out of the city for more than a day or so, they'd have heard from him at least once. And he'd been acting weird for weeks. Hiding something. The odd disappearance only strengthened their belief that something was wrong.

Pollux shook his head. "It's getting weirder and weirder, isn't it? Lynx is never gone this long."

"I don't like it." Castor didn't like a lot of things when it came to his uncle – Lynx's father. Sure, Castor was a Dragon just like the rest of the family, but that didn't mean he was under any illusions about the sort of people he was related to.

Yuri Kovalenko wasn't a good man. Their cousin Lynx, on the other hand, was. Spoiled, entitled, and sheltered, yes, but *good*. That combination never ended well.

"I don't like it either." Pollux reached into the cool chamber for a slice of simu-fruit.

Cantaloupe, Castor thought. The scientists did their best work, based on photographs and memories of the oldest citizens, but most of the engineered fruits tasted pretty much the same. Healthy but boring.

"I was thinking I'd go see Orion Leonias."

Pollux snorted and nearly choked on his fruit for a moment before he realized Castor was serious. "Orion Leonias? You want to go visit the Phoenix prince?"

Castor nodded. "There was something going on between him and Lynx at that council meeting a few weeks ago. I know you noticed it too. They aren't strangers, no matter what they pretended. Maybe Orion knows where Lynx is."

"And how exactly do you plan to get into the Phoenix compound with your head and your dick still attached?"

"I don't." Castor grinned. He'd been working on a plan while he rode the lift back to Cloud Level. "You know me better than that. You should also know the Phoenixes better than that. What's today?"

Pollux thought for a moment. "Is it Wednesday?" Castor nodded. "So you're going to try to sneak into the Lotus Room? Good luck with that. It's not much easier than getting into the compound itself."

The Lotus Room was a swanky cloud-level spa that catered to Phoenix triad lords and their most fervent suck-ups. Castor hated the place, which was fine, since Dragons weren't welcome there anyway. He figured he'd have to suffer the indignity for a few minutes if it meant getting some answers.

"Who said anything about sneaking? I've made a few very convenient friends. We both have. It's time to cash in."

One of those convenient friends was the owner of the Lotus Room's very party-drug-dependent daughter. Her tab usually ran higher than the contents of her purse, and she'd wanted more from Castor than his business for as long as he could remember. He would have no problem getting her to sneak him in during the Leonias family's coveted prime-time slot. He hoped.

Castor smiled. There was nothing he liked more than a good plan.

"ARE you sure this is a smart idea?"

Castor's friend Antila was spoiled and expensive, although not quite as expensive as one of the triad members themselves. Her parents owned a string of hard-to-get-into establishments, spas, clubs, restaurants—every one of them came with a waiting list and a pedigree check before entry. Castor had never seen her sober. Today was no exception.

"Ant, it's fine. I just want to talk to Orion, and then I'll leave." Castor gave her his best sexy grin. "Besides, I'm in here all the time."

Obvious lie. He hoped she was too bumped out to recognize it.

Antila wound her fingers together. "Papa hates when there are problems at one of his establishments. Bad press and all."

"I promise, I'll behave." *Irritating brat.* And to think just last week, Castor let her put off paying him the money she owed. No more favors. He ground out another one of his signature charming smiles and hoped it looked convincing. "I just want to talk."

Antila reached out and twirled a strand of his fiery red hair around her finger. Castor had to hold himself back from batting her hand away.

"Please?" He asked again.

"Fine." Antila gave a long-suffering sigh and flipped through the computer screen at the front. "I think they keep the schedule in here somewhere. It's where they usually book my pedicure times at least."

Castor didn't have time for her drug-addled brain to figure out a basic scheduling program.

"Here. Let me." He clicked through the different screens until he saw that Orion and his sister Cassiopeia were in the Hibiscus Room, supposedly getting mint steam facials. "Okay, I'll be back in five minutes. I promise. Just..." Castor gestured impatiently. "Wait here."

He doubted she'd even notice the time passing. Antila gave him a lopsided half-smile, already spinning on the reception chair and tracing the patterns of the ceiling tiles in the air with her finger.

Castor supposed it was his fault that half the young people of cloud city were perpetually strung out. It was still hard to feel anything but contempt for the lot of them. He checked the sign, then slipped down the thickly carpeted hallway in the direction of the Hibiscus Room, where he hoped to find some answers. The door slid open soundlessly. The room was occupied, but instead of two figures lying on the pillowed facial chairs, there was only one, definitely female. Definitely not Orion.

"Hello?" Castor said quietly.

He hoped it was the sister, Cassiopeia, and not some other high-ranking Phoenix woman who would most likely get him tossed into one of their compound's holding cells.

He was lucky.

"Castor Kovalenko? You *can't* be here right now," Cassiopeia whispered heatedly

She sat up from her reclined position, her slim body wrapped in a luxurious sheer robe. Castor could nearly see her curves through the material.

The signature genetically engineered Phoenix blue hair had manifested differently in Cassiopeia than her brother. While his was bright and electric, hers was dark like the deepest ocean, piled high on her head, shimmering and soft. She was beautiful. Beautiful and so, so off limits. The most off limits.

"You know how my father feels about you and your brother."

Castor did know. He was a Dragon, he was a huge flirt, and he was trouble of the most alluring kind to any kept daughter who'd barely seen anything outside her family's lush compound and the right well-mannered establishments.

A Kovalenko twin was enough to make any sensible father shudder in his shoes. Castor had always been fairly proud of that fact.

He'd run into Cassiopeia a few times since that night the Dragons and the Phoenixes had put down their problems to discuss the thief Yoru Katana—an enemy they could agree on for once. It was enough to know she wasn't much like most highborn girls. Cassiopeia was serious, intelligent, and quiet. Castor doubted she'd ever had a drug in her life. If she had, she certainly hid it well. And she didn't get them from him.

"I know what your father thinks of me. Of course I do. I'm not here for any of my usual reasons," he said quietly.

"I wouldn't know anything about your usual reasons," she answered primly.

Castor chuckled. "I've noticed you out and about lately, Miss Phoenix. You might not come to my type of parties, but I know you aren't anywhere near as sheltered as you seem. At least not anymore."

Cassiopeia sighed. "What do you want, Castor?" And then he saw it. Her eyes were weary, like she hadn't slept in days.

"What's wrong?" he asked.

"Nothing." Her face twisted. "It's just, Orion. He disappears a lot, but this time, he's been gone longer than usual. I'm worried."

"I was actually here to talk to your brother. You say he's gone?"

"Yes."

She looked at the floor. Castor was absolutely sure right at that moment. Two triad princes wouldn't disappear like that if there wasn't a serious problem. It just didn't happen. Ever.

"My cousin's gone too. Lynx. I was hoping you knew something about it."

Cassiopeia shook her head. "I'd only heard that Lynx was off on some vacation. I haven't heard anything about my brother."

"Lynx isn't on vacation. That's not like him, especially to take off without contacting anyone. Do you usually hear from your brother?"

"We don't talk much, but he'd tell me if he was going to be gone for more than a day or so."

"Do you think our families hid them somewhere? Because of Katana?" Castor's bad feeling was only getting worse.

"It would make sense with my brother," Cassiopeia answered. Orion was the first son, heir to the Phoenix throne. "Your cousin, though. Why would they hide him and not Leo?"

Good point. Castor was stumped.

The only thing he knew, the only thing that remained a constant in the whole weird situation, was his bad gut feeling that something wasn't as it seemed. It wasn't going to be easy to figure out what it was. Especially if his uncle or the Phoenix leaders had anything to do with it.

Castor's stomach sank.

Chapter Two

THREE WEEKS. Lynx had been gone for three weeks. One had been troubling, two a bit scary, but at three, Castor was about to lose his mind. Pollux wasn't faring much better. Neither of them had gone so long without talking to their cousin in their whole lives, especially not with the unrest that the bandit Katana had caused. No part of the situation was settling.

The twins had been checking with their contacts in the other levels of the city, but nobody had heard anything of Lynx's whereabouts other than vague rumors of vacations or drunken-party hazes, the same shit the press had been peddling for days.

Castor knew none of it was true. He and Pollux typically had to drag their cousin out for one single night of fun. Weeks of partying with no word to his family? Impossible.

The papers were out of control, of course. The stories ranged from the official city journalists' dutiful glowing society columns about Lynx's well-earned vacation and Orion's charity work in the outlying villages, to trashy tabloid reports of sleazy parties and salacious kidnappings.

The underlying whisper, the name that wouldn't be named, was Katana.

Nobody ever wrote *who* took the triad princes, only hinted that they'd been taken. Castor hated to take the rags seriously, but the real papers knew nothing and were paid to hock the party line. He was starting to believe that his cousin was in fact being held against his will, even if he'd always figured Katana was nothing but a ruse to cover underhand triad dealings. It was the best shot he had.

Other than Katana, the leads had completely dried up.

Castor had been messaging Cassiopeia for days. They couldn't use their regular accounts of course. Castor and Pollux were free to do whatever they wished, but Cassiopeia's guards checked her correspondence. She'd be questioned if there were too many messages back and forth with the troubled Dragon twins.

They'd opened a private encrypted chat on a secondary server. She was fairly certain nobody from her family would be bothered to hack the feed even if they ever did find it, so the twins spoke freely with her. He opened a message.

Have you heard anything from your brother today?

Her response came quickly. She must've been waiting to hear from them.

No. It's been way too long. I'm getting really scared.

Something's up around here too. Nobody is even talking about him. This is really wrong. We have to do something soon.

Castor hesitated. He didn't know how wise it was to involve Cassiopeia in anything that got too dangerous. He understood her fear, though. She must've been out of her mind with worry, wondering where her brother was.

We may have to meet. Can you get to our place unnoticed?

The screen was blank for a while.

Yes. I can manufacture an errand that will take me to your neighborhood. I can't stay away long. Will you be home in an hour?

Yes. We need to get to the bottom of this.

Castor put down his handset and called out.

"Hey, Pol. Cassiopeia is on her way here to talk. Get rid of anything too incriminating. She's going to try to come alone, but let's not take any chances."

They'd had a few clients over the night before to sample some new product. The sales pitch had gotten a bit interesting. Castor had already found a number of undergarments in cracks and crevices of the main living room. They needed to get rid of the rest of it, including anything illegal that might be lying around.

Neither of them could help Lynx from a safe and comfortable but very inconvenient Cloud Level holding cell.

"DOESN'T LOOK like I'd imagined it." Cassiopeia scanned Castor and Pollux's apartments with an eyebrow raised.

"And what were you expecting?" Pollux asked, his slow smirk only vaguely suggestive.

Bad idea, bro. Phoenix princesses are not the best thing to get involved with.

Actually, it was potentially the worst idea either of them had ever had. Right up there with the night they decided to take Lynx to Bottom City, where he must've gotten mixed up in whatever he'd been hiding from them ever since.

Cassiopeia shrugged her delicate shoulders under a thin gauzy dress.

"Den of iniquity? Drug house? At least a courtesan or two, lying about in an intoxicated stupor?"

Castor snickered, and Pollux laughed out loud.

"We don't quite run that level of operation, princess," Pol said without even a single guilty glance at Castor.

Pol cuffed her gently on the head. Cassiopeia looked at him as if nobody had ever done that to her before, probably because they hadn't. Who else would dare touch the likes of her if they wanted their fingers to stay intact?

"Have a seat." Castor gestured toward one of their leather divans. "Let's pool our info."

Pollux shot him a disapproving look, presumably for his short tone and lack of social niceties. Castor only rolled his eyes. He didn't have time to play socialite. He wanted to find Lynx. Cassiopeia wanted to find Orion. They had work to do.

"So your brother's been gone..."

"Three weeks. Or nearly so," she said quietly. "I've tried to talk to father and Aries, but they both keep shushing me. I'd swear on anything, they know something that I don't."

"Lynx has been gone that long too. Exactly. There has to be a connection. What do you think it is?"

Cassiopeia shrugged. "Maybe they know where Orion is and your cousin as well. Maybe both families know, and they don't want the people to find out."

"Why not?" Pollux asked.

Castor wanted to roll his eyes. Pollux was smarter than that. Must've been the hangover from the bump the night before. It had been pretty strong shit.

"Why do you think, Pol? Orion has slipped the grip of the great Phoenix lords, or maybe someone has taken him from under their sharp gazes. How do you think that info would reflect on them in the public eye?"

"Bad things happen, don't they?" Pollux murmured.

"Not to people like us," Cassiopeia said quietly. "At least not publicly. That's why my father and your uncle were so eager to get to the bottom of the Katana mess. They need him gone. He makes us look bad. Weak."

She looked uneasy. Castor didn't know why, but he filed it away in his head to think about later.

"And having missing sons looks pretty bad too, I'd imagine," Pollux agreed.

Castor nodded. "Are we all agreeing that something's not right here?" Cassiopeia nodded at once, Pollux a bit slower. "Okay, so then, what's the next step?"

Pollux shifted in his seat. "I put word out with my Bottom City contacts a few days ago. They'll come to me with any rumors."

"And have they *given* you anything?" Sometimes Castor wanted to strangle his brother. That bit of information would've been useful to know.

"Yeah, but I figured it was nothing."

Seriously. He exchanged looks with Cassiopeia. Castor imagined their impatient faces mirrored each other. Orion's sister didn't seem to have much more patience for anything than he did.

"And what did they tell you?"

Pollux shrugged. "Lynx has reportedly been seen with Katana. Supposedly he has Lynx and Orion held captive somewhere out in the ruins."

"Didn't you think that might be a good thing to tell us?" Castor thought he might explode.

Pollux shrugged. "They blame everything on Katana, don't they? There's a new rumor about him every day. As far as I'm concerned, until I see him with my own eyes, he doesn't even exist. He's just a convenient and well-placed ghost."

"Yes, but when the rumor involves our *cousin*, you tell me, Pol. Even if you think it's bullshit."

Pollux grumbled. "Fine. Well, then, Katana has been 'seen' with Lynx in Bottom City. I told you."

If Castor wasn't so anxious to spring into action on the finding Lynx front he would already be planning his strangling technique.

"I thought you said Katana supposedly had Orion too?" Cassiopeia asked. Her voice came out sharp and high.

"Who knows? The rumors are always vague and embellished. half the time there isn't any truth to them at all. Maybe most of the time. Like I said, until I meet this guy and have his blade against my neck, he's not a real problem."

Castor didn't want his brother to scare Cassiopeia. *"Pol."*

Cassiopeia cleared her throat. "I think we treat Katana as if we assume he's real. Like you said, he could be a total rumor, but he's also all we've got. I think we should put out more feelers. Look for him. Have you exhausted all of your Bottom City contacts?"

She turned to Pollux and stared at him directly with her intense luminous eyes.

He looked flustered. "Not yet. I'll get in touch with the rest of them. See if I can dig something up."

Pollux, who'd had his mouth, and who knew what other parts, attached to at least four different people the night before, nearly stuttered.

Castor tried not to laugh. *Seriously?*

Cassiopeia only nodded. She was either oblivious to Pollux's obvious and embarrassing crush on her or trying to avoid bringing it to any more attention.

"Thank you. Maybe we can work a bit harder on our

families too – the servants, suppliers. Someone in one of our compounds will know something."

Pol scoffed. "And they're going to tell you?"

Cassiopeia mumbled something that sounded like 'amateur.'

"They'll tell me. Perhaps not on purpose, but I had to have ways of learning what was going on in the world all these years. I'm not exactly useless."

Pol bowed. "My apologies, Princess. My brother and I will await your news."

Castor nearly laughed out loud. Cassiopeia frowned daintily. "I'll get right on it, then."

"JAFFA, Binny's crying again. She hasn't had anything to eat since last night."

Jaffa's gut twisted. He gritted his jaw and turned in the semidarkness of what passed for their apartment, trying not to look as worried as he was.

"Didn't you two have that basket of simu-fruits left from yesterday?"

Please let them just have forgotten about it.

Arlis shook her head. "That was the day before yesterday, and we ate them already. They're all gone."

Of course.

About a year ago, Jaffa had inherited two charges who'd insinuated themselves into his life and the small, abandoned clothing shop Jaffa had been squatting in for years. In the space of months, he'd nearly forgotten what life had been like before they were there.

The shop the little unlikely trio called home was in a crumbling, forgotten alley in an unused corner of lower midtown. Far enough from the center of town and low enough in the city, he'd likely never have to worry about it being snatched up and renovated. Also far enough from the populated areas that it separated them from the law enforcement officers who were typically on his tail.

Arlis was a couple of years younger than him; they'd celebrated her eighteenth birthday a few weeks before. Binny, her little sister, was only thirteen. They'd both learned to steal rather quickly under his reluctant tutelage, and they contributed food and clothing and even little decorations for their small home.

Sometimes the girls were a pain in his backside, but they'd become family since the day he'd rescued Binny from a patrolman who was about to take her to the shelter where she'd be separated from her sister.

The girls' parents had disappeared nearly three years ago, or at least they thought it was about that long. They had no clue where they'd gone or if they'd ever return. Jaffa was the closest thing they had to a parent, even if he was barely older than Arlis. He had to take care of them.

"I guess we're going to have to go out again today. Do you want to take the morning shift?"

Arlis nodded. They rarely worked together. He didn't want them to be connected to him in public, and two of them working any market drew more attention than one.

Arlis' sweet face and nimble fingers managed to procure bread from the bakers' first batches and simu-fruits from the greengrocers, while he was more suited to close work—stealing the money that kept them going longer than a few meals.

"I'll stick to the west quadrant today. Lower level."

Jaffa nodded. It was always a good idea not to hit the

same areas too many times in succession. Wouldn't want your face to get familiar.

"Be safe. I'll stay here with Binny."

IT ALWAYS FELT like forever when Arlis or Binny were out scrounging for free food—well, free as in stolen. It wasn't safe to take handouts in lower Metrolevel. Plus, the fewer people any of them made eye contact with, the better.

The girls were pretty sure they'd been chipped at one point. They didn't come from the streets like Jaffa did. They'd lived in a nice, clean apartment with their parents until the night their parents had disappeared and never returned.

Jaffa felt guilty for introducing them to his life. But they had to eat. Everyone did. And it was better for them to be together than for Binny to be in a home somewhere and Arlis off on her own.

He played a game with Binny while they waited. They'd found a few decks of antique cards, and her and Arlis had taught him some games. They'd beaten him soundly at first, but Jaffa was a quick learner, smart even though he'd never been educated. It didn't take him too long to pick up the tricks, but he still let them win. Most of the time.

Jaffa breathed a big sigh of relief when Arlis returned, two bags of various foods strapped to her back.

"Everything go okay?" he asked.

She smirked at him. *Brat.*

"Of course. I know better than to let some Dragon lord catch me trying to snatch his wallet." She'd been teasing him mercilessly about that since the day he told her. "Let's have breakfast, and then you can lift a few cards from the pretty ladies at the market to keep Binny here in berries for the rest of the month."

She reached out and ruffled Binny's hair. Binny grumbled but smiled at her sister.

Arlis dragged out her haul—fruits and pastries and even a few sausage sandwiches. It was hard not to shove all of it in their mouths. While Jaffa and the girls did pretty well with what they could get, they were hovering on the edge of hunger most of the time. Food was rarely guaranteed, and it always came with the threat of a heavy price.

The three relaxed for a while and let their meal settle before Jaffa hauled himself to his feet. He wasn't full any longer. He could never operate on a full stomach. It was time to do some real work.

He slipped out of their home after checking to see that the alley was empty, like he always did. They had a pile of old crates that they slid in front of the door when they were gone to make the place look as unkempt and empty as possible.

Jaffa moved the crates and checked once more to make sure the coast was clear. He walked, seemingly unconcerned, into the middle of Lower Midtown's city center, where all of the public lifts were located.

There wasn't any decent money to be had in Lower Midtown. Most of the inhabitants of his level were servers and butlers, people who kept the well-oiled Cloud Level functioning. He needed to get up to the Metrolevel Market. Jaffa thought of his near brush with the law a few weeks ago. He didn't like that Dragon, but he'd been pretty easy to give the slip to. Jaffa hoped he didn't run into any trouble again.

Don't jinx yourself, moron.

He crossed both sets of fingers before he slid into the

crowded public lift that let out right in the middle of the Metrolevel Market.

THE MARKET WAS no less crowded than it was on any other day, filled with the same array of faces and voices, smells and sounds. Jaffa was comforted by the familiarity. He'd been there so many times, done the same things over and over again.

It was a routine he could nearly do with his eyes closed. But he knew at the same time it was never a good idea to get too comfortable. Comfortable usually ended with a hefty stint in prison or death—two unfortunate possibilities that Jaffa seemed to encounter in his line of work far more than he'd like to.

After a few minutes, he had a perfect target in sight; a loud, blustery merchant with a fat stomach and bulging hip purses. Jaffa figured he and the girls could eat off the contents of one of those purses for months.

He crept closer, nonchalant, trying to blend in with the crowd, and slowly got into place between two stalls right next to where the merchant was spouting off something about his new bamboo garden. Jaffa reached out with his knife, small but sharp enough to cut through any strap or cord without tugging. He nearly had it and....

"*You* again."

A strong arm grabbed onto his midsection from behind. Jaffa struggled, but he was whisked into the back passageway of the market, away from the eyes of the public. He and his captor were surrounded by crates and carts full of packing material. Nobody would see if something happened to him. Didn't matter if they did. Nobody cared about the likes of Jaffa Sharp.

"Didn't you learn last time?"

Learn? The only lesson Jaffa had ever learned was that if he didn't steal, him and the girls couldn't eat. He struggled in the strong grip, turning to see who had him. He sighed when he caught sight of the flame-red hair and pale skin quickly turning an angry shade of pink. Of course. Only he would have the bad fortune of running into the same high-born jackass twice in one month.

"I wasn't going to harm anyone," Jaffa said with a sigh. "Why'd you stop me? That merchant has plenty more money where that came from."

He chuckled. The Dragon had the nerve to *laugh* at Jaffa. "If I'd have left you go, you would already be in shackles. Dorian Cornelius might be stuffed and oblivious, but his head of security is not. Best to stay away from him."

"I *will*. I promise. Just let me go."

Jaffa's protestations only earned more laughter. Then the Dragon's grip around his waist tightened. He got a hold of one of Jaffa's wrists with the other hand, holding tight so Jaffa couldn't squirm away.

"Time to come with me. I owe the police a bit of a favor." The Dragon finally let go of Jaffa's waist but began to pull him along, not very gently, by the wrist.

Jaffa panicked. The girls would never know what happened to him. He'd probably get conscripted into a work crew and disappear somewhere in a smelly garbage dump in Bottom City. He said the first thing that came to his mind.

"You don't want to do anything to me. I'll be missed if I'm gone."

"By who?" At least he stopped walking and turned, one vibrant red eyebrow lifted.

Jaffa thought fast. Who were all the pretty cloud-level richies afraid of?

"Yoru Katana," he spit out desperately. "I work for Katana. If I disappear, he'll find out who's responsible and take revenge. I doubt it'll be pleasant."

Jaffa was pleased with himself. At least until the Dragon smiled. "Well, that works out perfectly if I do say so myself. I'd like to discuss a few things with this Katana person myself. Take me to him."

Awww seriously? Shit.

"I don't—I'm not sure where to find him."

The Dragon's smile went sly. "You said you worked for him. You have to have some method of contact. I'm a very patient man. I can wait."

Jaffa sighed. He'd gotten himself into it this time, hadn't he? "Fine. I'll take you to Katana. We're going to have to go to Bottom City."

Maybe the thought of Bottom City would be enough to turn off the Dragon. Wouldn't want that perfect skin to get clogged up by the dirty Bottom City steam, would he?

"I figured as much. That's not a problem." *Of course he's okay with it.* Jaffa tried not to panic visibly. "We're going to take a little detour to pick up my brother, then I'm ready to go. Do whatever you need to do to contact your boss. I'm fairly sure you know what will happen to you if you're not successful."

Jaffa cursed to himself. How was he supposed to produce someone nobody had ever seen? He hoped that he could at least get the two high-level morons to Bottom City and lose them. This Dragon seemed to be quite a bit more wily than most, but he was still rich, and most likely, that meant stupid enough for Jaffa to trick.

He hoped.

Chapter Three

"THIS WAY," Jaffa muttered. His brain was working over-time, trying to come up with a plan on the fly. He had to lose his captor down below, there was no other choice, but it had been months since he'd ventured to Bottom City.

He only hoped he remembered it well enough to give Dragon boy the slip. The thought of what would happen if it became obvious that he didn't in fact know anything about Katana made him shudder.

"No, I said we're going to pick my brother up first. Come. Nobody will question your presence on Cloud Level if you're with me."

Exactly what he wanted. A trip to pristine, stuffy, Cloud City, inhabited by half the people he'd robbed in the past and the touchiest quick-trigger security guards in the whole city.

Jaffa cringed inwardly. "I'd prefer to wait here. Cloud city isn't my most desirable location."

"Do you honestly think I'm that stupid?" Castor snorted. "I have hand ties. I won't use them if you behave."

"You're not the police."

Jaffa was graced with an exaggerated eye roll. "I'm a Dragon. That means quite a bit more in this city than some meaningless badge."

He was annoying. Annoying *and* rather full of himself, but right.

Jaffa's captor withdrew a device from his pocket and pressed a few buttons.

"Hey, I found someone who can get us to Katana. You home? What do you mean—" He huffed out a loud breath and rolled his eyes again. "You really think this is a good time for that? She's out of your league. Leave it. I have someone who can take us to...*fine.*"

"Are we going to collect your brother?"

The dragon gritted his teeth. He looked annoyed. "No. Just take me to Katana."

Jaffa was immeasurably glad that he only had one high-born pain in his ass to ditch instead of two. Still. It was gonna be a challenge. He led the dragon to an outside lift, one that most people never went to, certainly not one that his royal red-headed highness would use or even know about.

The lift was rusty, out of repair, and usually made noises like what Jaffa imagined some dying ancient farm animal sounded like, but it would land them in a part of the Bottom City market where he'd been before and figured nobody in their right mind other than him would be familiar with. The perfect place to lose a cloud citizen. Especially an arrogant one who seemed awfully sure he'd be fine amid the squalor and danger down below.

"Where are you taking me?"

He hadn't expected much talking from his captor once he got his way. Jaffa was momentarily startled.

"The lift I use most often."

"No lift that I've ever seen before is in this direction. Are you sure you're not dragging me into a dark corner to kill me?"

"Maybe." Jaffa shrugged.

Truth was, he had little skill in actual combat and was better suited for running. Probably not best to tell anyone that.

The dragon had the gall to laugh. *Laugh.* He was probably right to laugh, but still.

"Don't get too ahead of yourself, kid. I'm not in the mood for hand-to-hand combat. I won't be nice."

"I told you I'm not a kid," Jaffa grumbled. "I'm twenty."

He doubted the dragon was much older than him, if at all. Plus, everything he said was annoying. Jaffa had food to steal, mouths to feed. He didn't have time to take some cloud-level moron on a tour of the less savory parts of New Seattle.

They walked in silence for long minutes, through thinning crowds and buildings that got less and less well kept as they left the center of town.

They were still in Metrolevel, so the city was passable, walls repaired and passageways mostly clean, nothing like the crumbling shop that Jaffa called home, but still. It must've looked pretty bad to a pampered socialite like his captor. He probably never saw a single sliver of garbage where he was from.

When Jaffa thought of home, he also remembered Binny and Arlis waiting for him. *Damn.* They'd be worried if he was gone too long. He needed to get back to them before he was missed. Hopefully with dinner. The last thing he needed was Arlis deciding to go out in search of him. She'd tried to rescue him once before, and that had nearly ended with both of them in a security holding cell for the night.

No, just get rid of the Dragon, and get home.

He had a lot of work to do before that happened, though. Hopefully the kind that didn't end up with him dead in a stinking Bottom City gutter.

"So, not-a-kid. What's your name?"

Jaffa hesitated. "Aaron," he spit out. He'd met an Aaron. Once.

"You're lying, and I'm not that stupid. Let's try the truth this time. Here, I'll start. I'm Castor Kovalenko."

Jaffa choked.

Of *course*. How could he be so goddamn stupid? Nobody else but him would have the bad luck of getting mixed up with one of the most dangerous citizens of cloud city. One of the *only* real dangerous citizens. *Shit.*

"I'm...Jaffa." He hesitated again, but this time, the Dragon was satisfied.

No, Castor *goddamn* Kovalenko was satisfied. *Shit, shit, shit.*

Jaffa wondered if it would be easier to kill himself right then and there. It was better than letting one of the wily Kovalenko twins use him and then get him arrested or sliced open in some bottom city slum, a thing that was quite likely to happen on his current course.

Jaffa didn't know much about cloud-level society, but everyone knew who the Kovalenko twins were—trained assassins, drug dealers, very high-level Dragon family members, not much further down the chain from the sons themselves. Seriously bad news.

I'm so screwed it's not even funny...

"So, Bottom City, huh? You think that's where we'll find our rogue?"

"Katana?"

Castor snorted. "Did you decide we were looking for someone else all of a sudden?"

Jaffa pretended he hadn't been mocked. As much as he knew, he should be terrified of Kovalenko, that he was in what might be the worst situation of his constantly precarious life, the most he could muster was virulent annoyance and an even more annoying mild awareness of Kovalenko's presence.

Like he could tell at any moment where Castor was standing, what his face looked like, pale and sculpted and surrounded by a fiery shock of hair. Jaffa wanted to punch something. He didn't have time. More story spinning to do.

"I have a meeting spot with Katana near the ruins," he told Castor. "He'll be there once I've summoned him."

"And how are you going to do that?"

Castor looked skeptical. By rights, obviously, since Jaffa didn't have a clue what the hell he was talking about.

"It's easy to get word to him. There are places. It's best not to talk about it." Jaffa wracked his brain.

He had to come up with something better than that, and quickly. The lift was old, but it would be mere minutes before they were in Bottom City. And he wasn't dealing with a stupid ball of highborn fluff like he thought when they'd first boarded. Castor Kovalenko wasn't going to be nearly as easy to lose as someone—anyone—else might have been.

"I know some parts of the ruins pretty well. Maybe I've seen this spot before. Where is it?"

Kovalenko was testing him, that much was obvious. Half the upper-city citizens had never even been to bottom level, let alone the outskirts by the dangerous ruins of the old city.

"You know the old church? The one by that broken highway ramp?"

The church marked the edge of Bottom City, where the overgrown ruins of Old Seattle encroached by a few feet every dank, dark year. There was a crumbly church still there, once stark white and festooned with diamond-shaped windows, but now covered in moss and brambles and slime. It was right next to a ruined park, an old broken arch of highway, and an ancient leaning street sign that read SEN with the rest ripped and dissolved away.

"The highway by the floating market?"

"No, not by the water. Uphill. There's an old park there."

Castor thought for a moment. "Yeah, I think I know it. Katana goes there?"

"He'll meet us there. I know a place to leave a signal."

Jaffa had no clue where Katana was, of course, or if he was even real, and he'd have to make up some signal that had zero chance of working, which was fantastic, but the old church was the only landmark by the ruins he could find with any confidence. And he was limber enough to disappear in the overgrown fountains of the old park and hopefully lose Kovalenko. The church and the park were a long walk from the section of the market where the lift stopped, but still in walking distance. He had to make it work.

The other direction led down to the stagnant wharves and the floating market, which was a lower level of the main market and if anything, even seedier, full of things for sale that Jaffa didn't even want to contemplate.

The water there was dark and thick with sludge and slime, covered by miles of city above. That was possibly the worst part of Bottom City. The wharves were filled with pale bloated thieves and murderers, sewer dwellers who wouldn't think twice to slit his throat, and for sure the throat of a highborn triad cousin. Jaffa cursed himself for forgetting. He could've lost Kovalenko in there with no trouble at all. Too late. He was committed to taking them on the long hike uphill to the damn church. At least he'd had some food earlier. He had a long walk ahead.

When the lift stopped at Bottom City, Jaffa steeled himself. The doors made an unearthly screech, nothing like the well-oiled ones in the middle of the city, and then they opened to a dark, quiet back alley near the market.

Bottom City wasn't any better than it had been the few times Jaffa had ventured down there before. It was still hot as the bowels of the underworld and smelled exactly like what it was—the moldy, steamy, rat-infested drainage point of every sewer in New Seattle with a refreshing overlying hint of dead putrid fish.

Jaffa gagged and tried not to show his discomfort. Wouldn't do to have the pretty socialite from Cloud Level realize he was scared.

"I need to go to that vendor in the corner. He'll get word to Katana that I need a meet."

"Okay, let's go." Castor turned to follow Jaffa in the direction he'd pointed.

Not the plan. How can I ditch him if he follows me? I can't. That's the answer. No ditching, lots of dying.

"Stay here. I need to talk to him alone. You draw attention." Jaffa gestured at Castor's bright hair.

"You're going to ditch me."

Honestly, at that point, Jaffa was mostly worried that if Castor followed him all the way to the vendor's stand, he'd realize he wasn't doing a damn thing there other than pretending to talk.

"I'm not. If you follow me, you're going to get us killed. Stay here."

Jaffa crept forward toward the stand, already eyeing the vendor. He looked seedy, like everyone in the Bottom City market did. Jaffa was scared to even look at what he was selling. He'd have to pretend to be interested in whatever it was.

"Whatdya want?" The gruff vendor said.

Jaffa pulled a few coins out of his pocket. "I'm trying to pull something on the Dragon prince back there. Just act like I'm telling you to do something."

The vendor accepted the coins warily. "This isn't gonna get me in trouble, is it? Not in the mood to get arrested today."

"No. You aren't going to see either of us again. Just make it look like you're messaging someone when I walk away."

"I'm going to need a few more coins if I'm going to be that helpful," he said with an oily smile.

Jaffa sighed deeply and dragged his last few pilfered coins from his pockets. He needed more money. That's why he'd been out in the first place.

Bastard Kovalenko...

"Just do it. I'm going to turn and walk away right now."

"You bought yourself a deal. Off with you."

Jaffa made his way back to his captor, hoping that the greedy vendor had sold his little lie to the Dragon.

"This way, Kovalenko," he said, trying to seem as unconcerned as possible. "He'll meet us."

"Call me Castor or Cas. I'm not much fonder of my family's name than you are."

"Fine. Castor. Follow me."

Jaffa crossed his fingers and still hoped that he'd find some lovely dark corner to dump his charge in so he could escape before they trekked all the way out to the old abandoned church.

Already the shifty gazes of the bottom dwellers were starting to get to him. Their big-eyed black stares and puffed-out white faces were creepy and harmless at best, dangerous at worst. Jaffa wasn't interested in sticking around to find out which. He felt like the people were getting closer, probably drawn in by Castor's bright hair and expensive clothing. They swarmed like subhuman maggots, drawn by shiny pretty things.

"Walk faster," Jaffa whispered. He didn't want the people to hear.

Castor picked up his pace to stay even with Jaffa's nearly panicked stride. "So, is Katana's hideout by this church you were telling me about?"

Jaffa scoffed. He hoped it was convincing. "Don't be stupid. He has meeting spots and signals all over Bottom City. I'm sure there are lookouts. By the time we get there, he'll already know I'm coming. Even I don't know where his hideout is. Nobody does."

He didn't want to dig his hole too deep, but the lie had to be big enough to convince Castor. Jaffa couldn't believe his bad luck. Out of all the Dragons and half Dragons in the city, he just had to get involved with a direct cousin, and one of the infamous twins with tons of underworld connections. Jaffa's life was as good as over unless his plan was successful.

"So, to the church?" Castor muttered.

Jaffa nodded. He led them away from the market and up a slippery damp hill toward the section of the old highway and the ruins outside of Bottom City.

·　·　·

THE RUINS WERE TERRIFYING. Dangerous. It wasn't a place for anyone, let alone a scrawny pickpocket and a cousin of the Dragon heir, no matter how wily and well trained. From what Jaffa had heard of Lynx, the cousin that was missing, he wouldn't fare well in the weed-choked ruins for minutes, let alone the weeks he'd been gone.

No wonder Castor's looking for him.

Jaffa had heard rumors the prince was out, on a vacation or some such thing. Obviously his cousin didn't believe the story. Didn't much matter. If the outlaw Katana really had the Dragon prince, he was most likely dead already.

They walked and walked, up more hills, slippery with never ending moss and slime, wet from the turbines of Bottom City and the perpetual darkness that covered everything.

"It's not too far from here," Jaffa eventually said.

It hadn't been very long – not as long as he'd remembered from when he was smaller. Of course, he'd been hoping to escape before they got there. He hadn't managed to do it yet.

He started to panic. He couldn't produce Katana or the lost prince. Castor Kovalenko would have him at the edge of civilization, somewhere easy to kill. Hopefully his original plan, the one where he got lost in the park and ran, would still work.

He'd have to run quickly. And not wipe out on the slime-slick hills on his way back down to the market and his chance to blend into the crowd. Jaffa told himself not to think about it. When it came time to act, he'd act. Until then, panic wasn't his friend.

"We just take a left turn at that corner, right? Actually, I know a shortcut. Follow me down this alley." Castor took

Jaffa's wrist and dragged him toward a dark, weed-choked opening. It looked ominous.

Of course he's been here before. Jaffa cursed his luck once again.

"Are you s—"

"Lynx!" Castor called out all of a sudden.

He took off at a run. He hadn't let go of Jaffa's wrist, so Jaffa was pulled along the dark alley, struggling and trying to break free.

This is not okay, not even a little bit. One of them is going to kill me. Dead Jaffa.

He tried to yank his arm out of Castor Kovalenko's grip one more time. All that happened was that he nearly tripped on the uneven Bottom City pavement.

Shit.

CASTOR PICKED UP HIS PACE.

"Lynx!" He shouted again, trying to get his cousin's attention.

It was him. Zero doubt. Most of his hair was obscured by a hood, but one tell-tale deep-red shock stuck out from beneath the fabric. Besides, after years of combat training together, Castor knew how Lynx moved. It had to be him. He called out one more time. The figure froze, and so did another one walking right in front of him.

Castor put one hand on his fusion pistol and used the other to drag Jaffa right up to Lynx. "Where have you—"

Lynx motioned for him to be quiet. "You can't be here, Cas," Lynx muttered.

"What do you mean, I can't be here. I came to freaking rescue you. Is this Katana?" Castor turned to the shadowed figure. "I have one of your men, we can make a trade. Better yet, Lynx, we can take him to your fath—"

His cousin held up a hand. "No, Cas. It's not like that. This is Katana, but I'm safe with him. He'd never hurt me."

Lynx was whispering, like he didn't want anyone to see them. Castor followed suit, since he figured a quick exchange was better than a big scene, but...

Wait. Did Lynx say he was safe with Katana? Was he *insane?*

"What are you talking about? You're *not* safe with him. He's a criminal."

Never mind that Castor had been questioning Katana's existence only a few days before. He clearly was real, and that meant his cousin was in danger. Right? Katana's hand flinched, and Castor tightened his grip on his pistol. But Katana merely raised his hand to lower the hood that had been obscuring his face.

At first all Castor saw was a fall of shiny black hair, but then his face emerged. Castor nearly dropped his weapon on the ground. Wrong color hair or not, he was Orion Leonias, missing crown prince of the Phoenix Triad.

How? That's impossible.

"Orion? You just told me Orion Leonias is *Katana*. Orion. *Katana.*" Castor wanted to hit something. He'd known things weren't quite right, but he'd gotten everything else all wrong. "I knew there was something weird going on at that damn dinner. What the *hell* kind of game are you two playing?"

Lynx clapped his hand over Castor's mouth. "Jesus, Cas. Are you ever quiet? We can't discuss this out here." Lynx made significant eyes at their Bottom City surroundings.

"Exactly where can we 'discuss this'?" Castor felt like a fool. He had no idea what was going on, but none of it made him look like anything other than a total asshole for caring about and searching for someone who clearly didn't want to be found.

"Follow me. Both of you," Orion said softly.

Even his quietest voice was authoritative. Castor had been planning to listen anyway. He wasn't returning to Cloud Level without some goddamn answers.

"It's a long story."

Chapter Four

"I'M GOING to need to you put these on. I'm sorry, it's a precaution."

Orion, no, not only Orion but goddamn *Katana*, tied some fabric around Castor's eyes. Jaffa struggled, trying to get away from Castor's grip. Castor wasn't about to give up his only piece of leverage, though, even if Lynx was a bit safer than he'd originally thought. Maybe.

To be honest, there wasn't much about the Phoenixes that he found any more trustworthy than a hacker thief. Castor figured it was best to keep all his bases covered.

"No way. You've seen me, you're coming too," Orion muttered softly to Jaffa.

"What do you mean, he's seen you? He works for you and hasn't seen you before?" It wouldn't be the weirdest thing that had happened since Castor woke up that morning.

Lynx laughed at that. Out loud. "Cousin, I believe you've been played. This kid doesn't work for us. I've never seen him in my life."

"You were lying to me?" The urge to hit something

washed over Castor again. If he could've seen where Jaffa was standing, he would've punched him.

"I'm a thief, and you were going to turn me in. What should I have done? Said yes, please, sir, and while you're at it, can you get me conscripted to some bloody border skirmish? What would *you* have done if you were me?"

Jaffa sounded frustrated and angry. Good. His lies got him into this mess.

Castor ignored the fact that it was actually *him* that got Jaffa into it. He'd been so annoyed when he saw the little shit stealing in the market that he'd grabbed him without thinking much beyond that step.

Castor shrugged, suddenly uncomfortable in the dark, with Katana, the lies, and pretty much his entire situation. "I suppose I'd have done the same thing."

"You're not going to kill me, are you?" Jaffa asked him.

"Me?" Castor muttered. "Maybe."

"Actually, I meant Katana. But anyone who wants to answer would be great." The poor kid did sound nervous.

"I'm not in the habit of killing people," Orion said. Castor heard the smile in his voice. "C'mon. This way. We have a bit of a journey ahead of us."

They walked for what seemed like ages before they were helped into some sort of vehicle. Lynx helped Castor find a handle. He could only assume Jaffa was led to one too.

"Hold on," Lynx said. "These old things kind of haul ass, and I'm not the best driver."

Castor felt a vague rumble beneath him accompanied by a whirring noise as they lifted off the ground. He nearly fell off his seat when the vehicle leaped to life and made a sharp turn.

"Where are you taking us?"

"To my supersecret villain lair, of course," Orion answered.

Lynx laughed, and Castor was pretty sure he heard a kissing noise. "Quit being a smartass."

Teasing? Kissing?

My cousin really isn't scared of him.

And wait a second. Since when is—

Castor remembered how Lynx had been ass-flipped over some guy right before he'd disappeared. Orion? Orion Leonias, the prince of the Phoenix triad and apparently also some infamous masked vigilante, was Lynx's guy? Impossible. Course, quite a few impossible things had already happened. Why not add to the party?

"What the hell is going on here? Seriously. I need some answers."

"Soon, Cas," Lynx's voice came from in front of him. "Let's get to somewhere safe."

THEY SPED ALONG, chilly wind blowing in their hair for a few long minutes before Lynx spoke up. "You won't be able to find a path out to this point from the city. You can take your blindfolds off if you want."

Castor whipped his blindfold off, but beyond trees and darkness, there wasn't much to see—just old cracked streets and buckled sidewalks black with mold, chunks of old buildings, and trees, lots of trees, dark, stunted, and leafless but covered in swathes of low-hanging moss and ferns. The trees shot out from old buildings, splintered and skeletal and covered what used to be patches of sky.

Now everything was blackness.

New Seattle glowed like a safe haven in the distance, so far away he could barely see it. Castor shivered. He'd never been so creeped out in his life. He scooted closer on the bench seat to Jaffa, who probably didn't like him much, but Castor imagined a warm human body in a sea of creepy darkness was welcome even if it was the guy who got him in so much trouble.

"Where are we?"

Lynx rolled his eyes. "In the ruins, obviously. Just a bit further out than you and Pol ever traveled. Rion and I live out here now."

"I suppose asking why is a waste of time."

Castor was starting to think he'd never really known Lynx. The cousin he thought he knew was terrified of the ruins. He would've have never aligned himself with someone like Orion Leonias either, Phoenix or thief.

"We'll tell you," Lynx answered. "But you're going to have to be patient. It's quite a bit further still."

THEY CONTINUED, up hills and down others, through canyons of old wrecked brick and metal shrouded in never-ending trees and slick dark moss. Once Castor could've sworn they were over water, but everything was so black that he couldn't be sure. Only a stiffer breeze and the faint smell of marine life made the place feel any different.

"Are you freaked out?" Jaffa whispered.

He sounded like he probably didn't want to be talking to Castor, but a person was a person and the poor guy had to be terrified.

"Lynx won't hurt us. I've known him my whole life."

"How about the other one?" Jaffa said.

"We can hear you," Orion said dryly. "And you're safe. Unless you take our location to one of our parents. Then we might have to kill you."

Lynx let out a cackle. "He's joking."

Castor wished he could see Jaffa's face in the dark. He felt marginally better watching his cousin joke around but only marginally. And he had to imagine their little thieving charge didn't feel better at all.

Castor felt the momentary urge to protect him. And then he rolled his eyes at himself in the dark.

Don't be a moron.

IT WAS like they were flying into some sort of void, the blackest of space, with nothing around them but cold air and damp. It was disorienting and it got weirder the further from the city they got.

Castor found himself gripping the safety handles on the transport, like it would keep him from flying out into nothingness.

He was nervous but no longer scared. He didn't trust Orion, even less now that he knew the Phoenix bastard was Katana as well, but he trusted Lynx with his life—at least the Lynx he'd always known. Castor told himself that he still could trust his cousin, that Lynx was the same man he'd always been, even if he seemed completely different. He could only hope he was right.

"Nearly there," Lynx said as they crested another hill. So far from the city, it was even quieter.

The distant glow had long disappeared, and their transport glided silently through near blackness shrouded by even more blackness with trees and old looming buildings.

"How did you even find this place? I can't see a damn thing." Castor wondered if it was a good idea to voice his weaknesses, but he figured he was already far away from the city

"Old maps and compasses," Orion answered. "It would've been nearly impossible without them. Now, we kind of know our way around. You'll see over time."

They slid into what seemed as if it was once an office compound. It was dimly lit by a few tiny outdoor lamps attached to what looked to be a low, flat mountain of concrete. It was creepy and strange, like something out of a book he'd read in school as a child. New Seattle was compact and vertical, nothing like this sprawling mass of blocks scattered on a sea of cracked concrete and scrubby bush.

"What *is* this place?" If he hadn't watched Seattle fade into the distance, Castor would've thought he'd landed somewhere on another world.

"It used to be a huge computer company. One of the biggest in the city. Remember reading about the old tech giants in history class?"

"Yeah, I do. Didn't the Chimeras rise from one of those companies?"

The Chimeras were one of the old extinct triads, the ones who'd started the war with the Sphinx Triad that had burned the sky. Castor's entire generation had been taught to hate them for what they'd done.

"That's a rumor. It might be true, but we'll never know." Orion shrugged. "I've learned not to believe anything we were taught in school about the history of Seattle. Most of it was triad propaganda."

Their transport pulled behind a gloomy old block of grayed concrete that had probably once been white. There were dark squares of window sunk like old hollow eyes into the side of the building. They all stumbled off onto cracked concrete.

"This place was a gold mine, though. We found it a

couple of weeks ago. It's remote enough that nobody from the city will ever find it, and it has tons of old parts and pieces lying around that I can build computer systems with. Ancient, but still useful."

"Why are you out in the ruins building computers?"

As far as Castor was concerned, Orion was squandering his cushy, perfect lifestyle. Lynx too for that matter. They'd had wealth, comfort, and status handed to them at birth. What were they *doing*?

Orion glanced around and then cocked his head. "C'mon. In here. Lynx and I will explain."

Castor followed and so did Jaffa. His little thief didn't look very comfortable. Castor bet that he'd run if he thought he had any chance of making it back to the city alive. They'd gone too far, though. Jaffa was lost if he tried to make it on foot. He had no choice but to trust Orion and Lynx. Neither of them had a choice.

THE BUILDING WAS big and cavernous, darker even than outside, and it smelled odd—like old stagnant air probably. Jaffa didn't know what that smelled like, but he remembered hearing stories about archaeologists getting fungus in their lungs from old shut-up tombs. His palms started to sweat. He wanted to get out. Jaffa shivered in the darkness.

"Not much further," the one with the red hair said.

Dragon, obviously, but oddly soft. He seemed nicer than the other one, the one who was in charge. That guy kind of freaked Jaffa out, to be honest. He didn't want to piss him off, figured that would be the worst thing he could do to make this bad day a hell of a lot worse, so he continued to follow and kept his mouth shut.

They were led into a small room, much warmer than

the others they'd passed by and actually lit with little clusters of energy-efficient lamps. It wasn't exactly a luxury apartment, but it was actually quite a bit better than Jaffa's own little hijacked store.

"Here," Lynx gestured. "Sit."

Orion opened his mouth to speak, and Jaffa jumped a little. The scarier one. Katana. Orion. Whatever. He knew that was a Phoenix name, and Orion was clearly a cloud-city citizen with his perfect skin and long fall of shiny, well-trimmed hair, but he was scary too, just like Castor.

Jaffa hadn't had the best of luck today. Figures he'd get tangled up with the few people from up top that he couldn't easily outmaneuver.

He obviously didn't want to be there, but he was smart enough to know he had no way out. His life was in the hands of two very young, and apparently very dangerous, triad sons. Or outlaws. To be honest, Jaffa wasn't sure any longer which one they were. Or which one was worse. The redheaded guy seemed nice, but it was always the nice ones, right? Besides. He was related to Castor. Not a good sign.

"First of all, you need to calm down." Orion pointed at Jaffa. His heart flipped unpleasantly. "Unless you draw a weapon on me, I'm not going to hurt you, okay? I mean it."

Jaffa nodded. His usual powers of speech seemed to have left him.

"Let's start with the basics." He looked at Castor. "Everything they taught us was wrong—all the things we've been lead to believe about the triads, about our families, about the past. It's wrong. At least most of it."

"What do you mean?" Castor asked.

He raked his hand through his hair until it stood up. Jaffa wished he knew what the hell was going on and when it was going to be over so he could just, *ugh*, get the hell out of there.

"There was a war between the Chimeras and the Sphinxes. At least I think there was; that part we can't disprove. But they didn't scorch the sky permanently. Maybe not at all. That's on our families. The Dragons and the Phoenixes."

Jaffa had never been to school. He didn't know why the sky was black when it wasn't years before, or why they should care who did it. Apparently Castor was pretty shocked by the news, though.

"How? What did our families do?"

Lynx turned to his cousin. "You know Butt Ugly Mountain up in town square?"

Castor snorted. "Of course. That thing is so hideous. I can't believe the city council ever commissioned it or paid for it."

"Well, they didn't, exactly. It was a gift. I'm sure you can guess who from. Hint. Our families. And it's not just ugly. For years, it's been producing the cloud that covers everything for miles around."

Orion paced around the small room. Jaffa watched him, trying to unravel what he was saying. So the Dragon and Phoenix triads made the sky black *after* the conflict. It didn't make any sense.

"But why?" Castor asked, echoing Jaffa's thoughts. "I mean, it sounds like something they'd do, but for what purpose?"

"You already know the answer to this, Cas," Lynx said. "Think about what we're taught. What's the story? Why are the Dragons and Phoenixes so powerful?"

Castor's eyes grew wide. "Because they were the white knights who swooped in and patented the drugs that saved everyone in the city from the lack of sunlight." He jumped out of his chair. "Those bastards. It was all for—"

"Money." Orion shrugged. He looked disgusted. "Our families realized organized crime would do well for them, but that the real money and power was in—"

"Legitimate business. They just had to make sure their business was fail proof."

"Yes. So if they could keep the sky dark, then everyone had to take the drugs they were manufacturing and selling. The artificial light inside feels good, but it's not enough to keep people from turning sick and pale like the Bottom City people. They're not mutants or freaks. We'd all look like that without our families' medicine."

"So it was all for money?"

Lynx nodded. "Money and power. We have to stop it. That's what Orion has been doing. That's what I've been doing."

"Why are you out here, though? What happened?"

Jaffa grew angrier as Lynx told the story of the night he and Orion broke the ARC, the machine that was spewing blackness into the sky. How Orion's own family went after them, and Lynx was nearly killed. He couldn't believe their own families would choose money and power over their children. At least Orion's cousin let him go. He wasn't going to do the same for Lynx—it was good that Orion was fast enough to get them both out.

Wait, why do I care about this?

Jaffa had been about to volunteer. He wanted to charge the Phoenix compound and take the evil empire down...but why? He forced himself to sit back and be rational. This was about getting away from these people, not joining their suicidal cause.

"So both your fathers know about the machine, and Aries," Castor asked.

"I'd imagine more than just that. It's a tightly guarded secret, but they had to keep it up, even as badly as they had. I'd imagine the whole inner circle knows. Not us. Not my sister. But I'd be surprised if Leo doesn't."

"Fucking hell," Castor ground out. "What now?"

"The ARC's been down for weeks. The cloud should be dissipating, but it's not, and we don't know why. We haven't been able to get medicine to the Bottom City children for days now, because the entire police force is looking for us. I need to steal another shipment, but I'm sure Aries has tripled his watch. It's not a good time for either of us to be in the city. I don't know what to do."

"What if you had help?" Castor asked.

Moron. Of course you want to help them. You don't have anything better to do other than sit around and be rich.

Jaffa tried not to let his irritation show in his face. Must be nice to have the luxury to be superheroes, since they didn't have to scrounge around for food every day.

Orion shook his head. "I can't ask you to risk yourself like that."

"Did Lynx ask?" Castor rolled his eyes like it was all a big game.

Lynx laughed. "No. I pretty much forced my way in. He didn't want me around at first either."

Jaffa found himself opening his mouth. "I know quite a bit about stealing things. Castor's the first person who's ever caught me. I could help too."

Wait. What? Did I really just say that? It was like Orion and his damn noble cause had some sort of hypnotic power over him. *Take it back. Take it back.*

"What's your name again?" Lynx asked.

Lynx's voice was still kind, even when he talked to someone as insignificant as him. Nothing like he would've expected a Dragon prince to be.

"Jaffa. My name is Jaffa."

Lynx nodded. "What we're doing is dangerous, Jaffa. You don't even know us. Why do you want to help?"

I'm clearly insane. But then he thought about it a little more and started to realize that, no, he wasn't insane.

"Truthfully? What's about to happen in this city will be just as dangerous, and people like me and the girls I take care of, we're the insignificant types who usually end up dead. I'd like to bring them out here. They're quick on their feet and have fast hands. We help you. You protect us."

After he said it, he realized it was right. Nowhere was safe for someone like him if a war was about to break out. Stealing was stealing, and, well, at least they'd have shelter away from whatever was about to go down.

"You're really ready to just pledge yourself to our cause like that?" Lynx asked.

"You got food?" Jaffa countered.

"Of course."

"A safe warm place to sleep that probably won't be raided?"

"About as safe and warm as you can ask for people like us," Orion told him.

Jaffa nodded. "Then, yes. That's more than we had this morning."

"I don't think..." Orion started.

"Babe, they can help. We *need* help." Lynx covered Orion's hand with his own.

"Babe?" Castor snorted. "Has it progressed that far?"

Lynx slipped his fingers in between Orion's. "Yeah."

"Should've guessed." Castor grinned. "You've always

been the settling-down type. God, after what happened with that Celes—"

"*Cas.* Shut up. Seriously. That was another lifetime."

Orion ignored the cousins' banter. "You guys really want in? Both of you?"

"Of course. Like I'd pick Lynx's corrupt asshole father over you guys," Castor said. "Even before you told us what they've been doing, I'd have taken your side. Lynx is my family. His father isn't."

Everyone looked at Jaffa. "Yeah. I'm in. The girls will be too. We got nothing there to hold us but the constant threat of starvation."

Orion seemed to accept it then. He nodded slowly. "Okay, then I have a few more people you'll want to meet."

"There's more?"

Jaffa watched Castor's eyes bug out like he couldn't believe everything he was hearing. It was hard for Jaffa to swallow too, but not exactly surprising. Everyone knew the triads were corrupt. It was a bit of a shock just how exactly corrupt they were. Ruining an entire city and who knows how many miles around it just for money? What the hell could any of them do to fix it for good?

Orion led them through a few dark hallways until he got to a curtained-off doorway.

"This is the main living area. It's warmer in here. We think it must've been one of the cafeterias back when this was an office building. There are old ovens that actually worked once we hooked them up to generators, and the room is big and bright."

Orion held open a curtain and led them into a large vaulted room. There were larger collections of lamps all hooked to generators that hummed softly, and he was right. The room was warm. A bit too warm. Nothing like the climate-controlled perfection of the city. But something about it felt warm and cozy, like a real home.

He smiled. "We're still working on getting the temperature right. It goes from freezing to hot really quickly. The good part, though, is Vela's learning to cook."

A bright pink head popped up from where it had been hiding behind a counter. "You make it sound like cooking's all I'm good for, Rion. Thanks a million."

Orion chuckled. "Vela, this is Lynx's cousin Castor and our other newest recruit, Jaffa. They're going to need rooms. Do we have enough fabric to make more curtains?"

"Oh, fantastic. Cooking *and* sewing. Maybe we can get some children for me to watch too while you're at it."

"Well, about that..." Lynx grinned sheepishly.

"Arlis is eighteen," Jaffa smiled himself. "Binny's a bit of a handful, though."

It was hard not to get caught up in their camaraderie and familiar teasing. Walls he'd had for years had already started to disintegrate merely upon contact with Lynx and his friends. Jaffa almost felt like he had to hold it in, keep his guard up, be wary of giving his trust away. But it was hard when everyone else in the room seemed to have already decided to trust him.

"Fantastic," Vela muttered. Jaffa couldn't help grinning.

"Vela's really our tech expert," Lynx told them. "You should see what she's capable of."

Vela curtsied, pink hair and round cherubic face bouncing up and down.

Orion gestured to a huge guy who'd just ducked into the room carrying boxes of what appeared to be water. "And this is Seth."

"Resident muscle." Seth winked at them.

Lynx rolled his eyes. "He's an amazing shot. He's our

main security expert. There's no way we'd get in and out of places safely without him."

"N-nice to meet you guys." Jaffa didn't know what else to say. He wasn't great at social situations. Come to think of it, he'd never been in a social situation before in his life. But for the second time in only minutes, he found himself *wanting* to have friends. Joining the rebellion was as good of a place as any to start, right?

"I'm going to have to go back for the girls," he said.

"And I'm going to get Pollux," Castor added. "I seriously don't think I'm going to have a hard time talking him into this."

Lynx snorted. "You don't have a hard time talking him into anything."

"That's why he's my brother."

Orion looked at Castor. "Listen, I think you two should live in the city. We can't have too many triad kids disappearing. Plus, it can't hurt to have some guys on the inside. We're going to need people who have access to at least one of the houses."

"I was thinking the same thing. I still want to bring him out here to talk to you. He needs to see and hear it for himself."

"Of course," Orion demurred. He turned to Jaffa. "Do you have many belongings to transport out here?"

Jaffa almost laughed. Belongings. Seriously. "I barely have the clothes on my back most days. The girls have a few things. Nothing we can't carry."

"It'll make things easier. Why don't I send Seth with you to help? Like I said, he's useful if you get into a pinch."

Jaffa nodded. The big muscle-bound guy made him nervous, but if he was on their side, well, that was a good place for him. Jaffa wouldn't want to be on the wrong side of that guy's fist. Ever.

"I say it's time to get moving. If you time it perfectly, the atmosphere controls will be set to darkness in the city. Perfect for slipping out unnoticed."

"Thank you, Orion. Really. You didn't have to take us in. We'll help as much as we can." Jaffa hadn't ever thanked anyone before either. The words felt odd coming out of his mouth.

Orion put his hand out and patted Jaffa on the shoulder. "I've been burned in the past. Badly. But you seem like a good guy. I'll see you when you return."

Chapter Five

———————————

JAFFA AND CASTOR headed for the transport vehicle with Seth in tow. Castor glanced over at him with a smile on his face. Not one of his sarcastic sly grins, but a real smile, one that turned him from aloofly and annoyingly pretty to breathtaking.

Jaffa's belly twisted pleasantly. He could barely believe the change from angry, self-righteous Dragon lord to teasing cousin and friend. It was uncanny.

This Castor was someone Jaffa wanted to talk to and laugh with and *touch*. He was attracted. He'd figured that out somewhere between the dark transport ride out into the ruins and Castor's soft smile only moments before.

Jaffa's hands itched to test the texture of his fiery hair, to see just how smooth his pale skin would be to the touch.

Jaffa shook himself out of it. He'd never wanted to touch anyone like that before. Hell, he'd never had the time or the luxury to bother thinking about anyone like that before, and the first person he managed to pick was Castor goddamn Kovalenko? The strange day was bringing all sorts of things out that he didn't know what to feel about.

No. I know how to feel. He's a Dragon. He'd kill me in a heartbeat to save any one of his highborn family members.

Of course, Jaffa would probably kill to save Arlis or Binny if he could too, so maybe he didn't blame the guy.

"You lied to me," Castor said with a surprisingly good natured laugh as they climbed back onto the transport, like he still couldn't believe someone had the balls to con him but he didn't really care. "You didn't know a thing about Katana."

"You were going to have me arrested."

Don't smile. He's still him, and you're still you, even if you did just somehow join the same side.

"True." Castor shrugged, like it was all part of a game.

Jaffa supposed a lot of things probably seemed like a game to someone who'd had a life like Castor Kovalenko. Castor smiled like they were already friends, the white of his teeth flashing in the gloom. Jaffa smiled back, disarmed by the joking. How things had changed in such a short time.

"Besides, you got your cousin in the end, didn't you?" Jaffa said. "That's what you were after, No harm, no foul, right?"

"And you got somewhere permanent to live with your sisters where nobody from the city can find you."

"Also true."

Jaffa didn't bother to tell him they weren't really his sisters. As far as he was considered, they were. He turned and stared out into the darkness, but he tried to keep his body casual.

If Castor wanted to act like it was all a big fun game, then Jaffa could do the same. He was right, though. Getting dragged into this may have been the best thing that had ever happened to Jaffa and his two girls. If they didn't end up getting killed by the triads, that is.

"Can we call a truce?" Castor asked. "Looks like you and I are on the same side now, and we might as well be friends if we're going to end up seeing a lot of each other. I don't like it when people hate me."

And he's a mind reader too.

"I think I can handle a truce," Jaffa finally said. It wasn't like he *really* had anything against the guy. They were both just looking out for themselves, after all. And they'd both gotten something good out of it. For now at least.

Castor stuck his hand out, and Jaffa reached for it. He was surprised by the warmth of Castor's palm and how the slide of his fingers made electricity tingle up his spine.

"Friends?" Jaffa whispered.

What's happening to me?

"Yes. Friends."

"GIRLS. WHERE ARE YOU?" Jaffa muttered into the dark empty store.

His heart raced. How could they have disappeared already? He hadn't been gone for more than a few hours. Twenty minutes was enough for them to get themselves into trouble on a bad day, but he'd hoped for the best.

"Arlis, Binny. Where are you? It's Jaffa."

Two pale faces peeked out from behind a pile of boxes. "Jaffa?"

Relief slammed through his body. "You scared the *hell* out of me. I thought you two'd been taken."

He reached out, and two thin, squirmy girls landed in his arms. Jaffa squeezed them. He kissed Binny on the forehead and Arlis on the cheek. She might end up taller than him soon enough. He couldn't believe how grown-up they'd become. He guessed it was for the best, with what he was about to ask them to do.

"Sorry, Jaff," Arlis muttered. "You were gone for a long time, and there were men walking around outside. We thought it was best to hide. You get anything good?"

Yes... and no.

"You were right, love. Listen, we're not going to stay here anymore. Something's about to happen in the city, and it's not going to be safe for a while. I need you two to pack your stuff up. We have a better place to go."

"On this level?" Binny asked.

Her world had become so small. She rarely even ventured onto the Upper Metro levels. The idea of some far-off corner of the ruins would sound like another planet to her.

"No. Not in the city at all. C'mon girls. We have to move quickly. There are people waiting for us."

They packed their bags hastily and slung them over their backs. Jaffa didn't even have time to feel bad about how few things the two girls had to call their own. He simply ushered them out of their sad little former home and into the dark streets of Lower Metrolevel Seattle.

"They're waiting for us at the south lift. Arlis, you lead. Keep a sharp lookout. Binny, you're in the middle. Stay between me and your sister."

Jaffa didn't know why he had an uneasy pit in the bottom of his belly. It should be no problem. Just a quick evening walk through the neighborhood to the lift he'd used a thousand times. No problem, right?

Still, they walked silently, watchful and careful, toward the south lift. Arlis must've felt it too. Her steps were quick and light, her movements studied but outwardly casual. It was the way she walked when she was following a mark.

Jaffa had trained her well. Hopefully their caution would be all they needed to get them to the lift. At least it was less remote than the one Jaffa had herded Castor onto earlier, which could be good or bad.

The trip was short, but there may still be people near it, headed out for the night or in after a long day of work. Three skinny, raggedy-looking street kids with packs on their backs would draw attention in a crowd of service professionals on their way home. If nothing else, they'd be tagged as panhandlers and taken in for the night to city holding.

They rounded the corner to the southeast square that held most of the main shops in their quadrant of Lower Metro. It was deserted. Nearly there. A small crash made all three of them jump, but a stray dog bolted out into the square and disappeared into the night. Thankfully, it was nothing.

Jaffa breathed a sigh of relief when they reached the lift and saw only Seth and Castor and another boy who was both the mirror image of Castor and somehow completely different—calmer, less tightly wound, nowhere near as fascinating.

As much as he felt weird about Castor—both an electric thrill and a belly-flipping unease at the same time—he got none of that from the brother. Jaffa liked him immediately.

Arlis, on the other hand, froze in her spot.

"That's Castor Kovalenko," Arlis breathed. "And Pollux."

Jaffa was taken aback. "How do you know about them?"

"How do you not?" She looked at Jaffa like he might have just crawled out from under some back-alley rock.

"I do, actually. Remember the Dragon who nearly caught me in the market?"

Arlis burst into quiet giggles. "It was one of them? Jaffa, they're *famous*. They've been all over the tabloids, even more in the past few weeks. They're rich, dangerous, *hot*." She had literal stars in her eyes. Jaffa was irrationally irritated.

"Yes. Dangerous. Mister Castor Kovalenko over there tried to have me arrested earlier today. Again."

Arlis's stars flipped to anger. "He did *what*?"

She stomped over to Castor and was about to raise a thin finger into his face before Jaffa caught up to her.

"Arlis, it's fine. We've settled it. Besides, if we hadn't, did you really think confronting him was a good idea?"

Her loyalty was both her best quality and her biggest weakness.

"Jaffa, this is my brother, Pollux. I assume those two are with you."

Castor and his brother peered curiously at the pair of skinny girls he called his only family.

"Yes. Castor, Seth, Pollux, this is Arlis and her little sister Binny."

"Ladies." Castor and Pollux both nodded respectfully, and then Castor gestured toward the lift.

"Thank you," Arlis said primly. She looked like she was about half a second away from either strangling Castor or launching her mouth into his face.

Jaffa had to hold himself back from laughing out loud.

***

"JAFFA, I CAN'T SLEEP."

Binny had wandered into his area of the main room rubbing her eyes. She'd never slept in a bed on her own, never more than a few feet away from him or Arlis. It had to be disconcerting.

"You want to come in here with me?"

"Yeah, thanks. Sorry, I feel like such a baby."

"Hey." Jaffa covered her up and let her squish next to him. "We've only been here a few nights. You have to get used to it still."

Binny was still a little kid in some says — street smart far beyond her years, but sheltered by him and Arlis as much as humanly possible. All the changes had to be hard for her.

"What's happening in the city? I don't really get why we had to come out here."

Jaffa sighed. He loved how loyal the girls were, how they'd packed up without question and followed a couple of dragon lords and their security guy out into the darkness. They had to be confused though. Especially now that they settling in was done and the waiting had begun.

"It's a long story squirt."

"Are you tired?" She raised her eyebrow in such a perfect carbon copy of Arlis it made Jaffa laugh.

"I suppose not. The triads, The Dragons and the Phoenixes, did something bad. They have a machine that's keeping the sky dark so they can sell the pills that make people healthy and make a lot of money. You know the ones we used to steal from the delivery trucks?"

"Yeah. That sucks." She made a face. "And we're out here because..."

"Because Orion and Lynx broke the machine and if the cloud starts to go away then there's going to be chaos in the city."

Binny nodded. "I get it. And people like us get trampled in the middle of it."

"Exactly."

"But if Orion and Lynx's family started it, if that's what made them so rich, why did *they* break it? Why are Castor and Pollux helping them?"

"Because our families suck," came a voice from the edge of Jaffa's room.

"Sorry. Did we wake you?" Jaffa asked. Castor usually went back to the city at night, but he'd been with Orion and Lynx too late and he'd decided to sleep for a few hours.

"Nah. It's too quiet out here. I couldn't sleep. Even Cloud Level has more noise."

Castor came over and perched at the foot of Jaffa's small bed.

"So, what, you're just sticking it to your parents for sucking?" Binny asked.

Castor chuckled. "My uncle, actually. Lynx's dad. But no, it's not just that. We know what they did was wrong and I think all of us feel a little bit responsible for fixing what our families did."

"Don't you miss all the fancy food and the nice parties?" Binny asked.

"Not even for a second."

Castor smiled and reached out to ruffle her hair. Jaffa had been shocked the first few days by how utterly sweet Castor and Pollux had been with the girls. There were these two *badasses*, and they looked at Arlis and Binny like the little sisters Jaffe knew they didn't have.

"Hey, Binns, I'm getting tired. Do you want to stay in here or try to fall asleep in your own bed?"

"Stay in here, please. I promise I'll get used to it but..."

Jaffa smiled. "It's okay, love."

"Hey, are you coming with me into the city tomorrow?" Castor asked. "I was going to go on a supply run."

"You want me to steal food?" Jaffa asked. He supposed the time for him to be useful had come.

Castor chuckled and ruffled Jaffa's hair like he had Binny's. "No, we're going to *buy* food. We've cloned a bunch of cards to draw from Phoenix and Dragon slush funds. They'll never notice the missing money, we'll get decent provisions. Win win. I just needed a bit of help and Pollux is going to stay visible at home."

Jaffa nodded. "I'll go."

He tried to pretend he wasn't thrilled at the prospect of going into town alone with Castor. Binny clearly didn't buy his act if her half-hidden grin said anything. Castor most likely didn't either. Jaffa blushed for probably the first time in his entire life. Great.

"I'll come get you before I take off in the morning."

Jaffa simply nodded.

IT WAS weird to be completely alone in the transport with Castor. Jaffa hadn't been alone with him since that night when they trekked down into Bottom City to "meet" with his boss Katana.

Every time he thought about how that could've worked out, he panicked a little bit. Jaffa had been so immeasurably lucky.

"You okay over there?" Castor asked.

He reached over and brushed Jaffa's Shoulder. Jaffa had been aware over the past few days how demonstrative Castor had become with him. Pollux too, although he tended to reserve the touches and hugs for the girls more than him. They were still both nothing like what he'd imagine Cloud City royalty to be like. Lynx and Orion as well.

"Yeah. I'm okay. Why?"

Castor shrugged. "You seem nervous."

"I guess I haven't left the compound since me and the girls got there. It'll be weird going back into the city."

"To the place where I caught you?"

Jaffa rolled his eyes in the dark. "Yes. The most embarrassing moment in my life. Twice."

"It could've been worse."

Jaffa had been thinking exactly the same just a few minutes ago. "It could've been way worse."

"So game plan for the market. We'll need to stock up on food mostly, but there aren't enough blankets and I want to get the girls a few things as well. Some games, maybe."

"They have you so well trained." Jaffa chuckled.

"Like you weren't out half the time stealing to keep them in food and clothing." Castor nudged him. "Don't pretend you don't love them."

"I do," Jaffa freely admitted. "They're not my sisters biologically, but they're still my sisters."

Jaffa also loved watching his two charges wrap the fearsome Kovalenko twins around their delicate fingers — not to mention Lynx, Orion and the others. The last thing they probably really needed out there were two teenage girls. But they'd welcomed them with open arms and treated them like they'd always been there.

"I'm sure they'll love whatever you pick out for them."

Anything Castor could get the girls with his uncle's vast reserve of black money would be a million times nicer than anything Jaffa felt comfortable stealing for them. And if nothing else, the thought was sweet. That Castor just wanted to make his girls smile.

.   .   .

THE MARKET WAS the same as it always had been, but it felt completely different. Jaffa used to look with a thief's eye — for people who were distracted, anyone who looked like they could afford to lose a few coins here and there.

It was hard not to see the things he'd spent a lifetime training himself to see. But he had actual *money* now. Or at least he had a high born Cloud Level citizen with money walking next to him like they were equals.

"Do you want me to wait behind the stall?" Jaffa asked when they got to the first place Castor gestured at.

Castor made a face. "No. Why?"

"I'm clearly not one of you." Jaffa gestured at Castor's general expensiveness. Even in an upper Metrolevel market, Castor stood out. Jaffa seriously hoped Castor had no intentions of going to the market in Cloud Level.

"So what? You're here with me. You're my friend."

Friend. That word hit Jaffa in places he didn't want to even think about. He and Castor were friends?

"Really?"

"Of course. We already discussed it." Castor brushed it off. "Now come help me pick some things that we can buy for Vela and Lynx to make for dinner. I have no idea how to cook."

"Like I do?"

Jaffa didn't have a damn clue. He was glad that Vela did, and that Lynx seemed to be taking an interest in it. He was mostly happy that for the first time in his life, he had regular meals to eat and that the girls did as well.

"Just... see what looks good."

Jaffa shrugged. "Sure."

They filled their cart with dried goods and some simu-fruits and vegetables, bottled drinks, and sweets for the girls — and Seth who had an outrageous sweet tooth.

Then Castor dragged Jaffa around to pick out gifts for the girls and even clothes for him, which made him blush.

"You can't always wear what you have on," was what Castor said as he draped shirts over Jaffa's arms that were far nicer than anything he'd even considered having. "Just take them."

By the time they'd loaded their transport and set back off into the darkness for the camp, Jaffa was exhausted. Exhausted and weirdly excited they didn't get caught somehow.

"Uncle will never notice. And if he did, he would've never figured me for the one who was spending all his cash." Castor made a face. "I think it's probably a good thing that he thinks I'm useless."

"You? Useless?"

"In our family, If you're not Leo, you're not... well, Leo."

Jaffa remembered hearing something of the sort from Lynx. Apparently, the perfect oldest brother Leo was the only Dragon who mattered to Yuri Kovalenko.

"I don't think you're useless."

Jaffa was insulted on Castor's behalf. And Pollux and Lynx. From what he'd seen, they were all smart as hell and dedicated to something they honestly shouldn't be bothered to even care about.

"Thanks, kid. I think you're pretty awesome too."

Jaffa sighed. "Someday, you're going to figure out that I'm not even a year younger than you and I'm definitely not a kid."

He heard Castor's quiet chuckle in the cool, dark air. "Nah," he said. "It doesn't matter how old you are. You're still a kid."

Chapter Six

"HOW WOULD you like to go out? We need some help and there are too many eyes on me and Orion right now." Lynx asked Jaffa one morning.

Well, Jaffa *thought* it was morning. It was disorienting out there in the ruins without the artificial sun and darkness to tell their bodies what they were supposed to be doing.

"Out?" Jaffa sat up at the breakfast table and abandoned the coffee he'd been nursing.

He'd been there for days and days and other than the market trip with Castor, he'd barely done anything other than eat, sleep, hang out with the girls, and develop a huge obnoxious crush on someone who was so far out of his league he might as well be on a different planet.

Jaffa couldn't help with the computers that Lynx, Vela, and Orion were always tinkering around with and he wasn't big enough or good enough with any weapon to run perimeter checks with Seth. He was basically their helpless ward. Or at least he *had* been. Now, he might finally be of some use.

"Yeah. Yeah, of course. How can I help?"

"We've been getting medication to the Bottom City kids but the transports we used to rob, the ones that go all over town? They've stopped them."

Jaffa remembered the transports well. He'd spent years filching medication from them for himself, and then for himself and the girls.

"How are they distributing the supplies now?" He asked.

Lynx shook his head. "I'm going to need you guys to work on that. We don't know since they've been a lot more careful about their communications since they figured Orion and I out."

"You guys?"

"I'm putting you on this with the twins. They know the triads, you're our master thief. You guys need each other."

Jaffa chuckled. "Master thief." He supposed the laughter was a little bit at the title, and a little bit of nerves at spending time with Castor again.

"You said nobody ever caught you until Castor? I'd consider that pretty impressive."

"He shouldn't have caught me either." Friends or not, Jaffa was still a bit sore about that day.

Lynx grinned. "Don't underestimate my cousins. They're pretty wily."

"I think I've figured that out."

The cousins played at being devil may care society boys, but they weren't. Not even a little bit. Jaffa remembered the intimidating Castor from the market that first day. *That* was the real him. Or the one who was sweet and caring with Arlis and Binny. The bumped out poster boy for Cloud Level excess seemed to be a complete façade. So yeah. He knew better than to underestimate the twins.

Lynx put his hand on Jaffa's shoulder. "You'd better get ready to go."

HE ONLY HAD to wait an hour or so until Castor and Pollux showed up at the camp with big grins and a huge box of treats for everyone.

Jaffa marveled at the difference between the Castor he'd met that day in the market — surly, aristocratic, and very superior — with the Castor he'd come to know only a couple of short weeks later. He was quick to laugh, ready for adventure, and he seemed to really love his brother and his cousin.

He also lavished more attention on Jaffa and the girls than any of them could've expected. Jaffa caught Pollux giving Castor knowing looks every so often. He also caught Castor looking at *him* fairly often.

Which Jaffa tried to ignore, if only for his own sanity.

It was too tempting to forget his precarious situation and spend way too much time and energy thinking about one rich dragon boy who was his first real crush and from an entire different level of the social atmosphere.

"Hey," Castor said to him after he'd greeted everyone and passed out treats to everyone and trinkets to Arlis and Binny. Castor nudged Jaffa with his shoulder. "I hear we're going on an adventure together today."

"With Pollux," Jaffa said quickly.

Castor laughed. Somehow he seemed to see right through Jaffa's attempts to put distance between them. "Yes, my brother is coming too. It'll be fun."

"Fun?" Jaffa was learning pretty quickly that nothing made Castor happier than sticking it to the man — the man in this case being his uncle that he hated — but fun seemed to be a bit of a stretch.

Castor slung his arm over Jaffa's shoulders. "Don't worry. We won't get caught. I'll keep you safe."

IT WASN'T until Jaffa had said goodbye to the girls and was speeding along in the darkness with Castor and Pollux that he really thought about what they were doing.

"How am I not going to stick out like a sore thumb on Cloud Level? Doesn't everyone up there know each other?"

Pollux chuckled, "Have you really never been up there?"

"Do you really not know how hard it is to get up there when you don't belong?"

Sure, Jaffa could've forged some identification that showed he worked for one of the rich Cloud Level citizens, gotten himself into the market, and tried his best not to get killed, but it wasn't worth it. Metrolevel had been good enough for him.

"It's really not that great. You'll see." Castor reached back in the dark and squeezed Jaffa's knee. "Most of the time, Pol and I are trying to find excuses to get out and come be with you guys."

"Right. Not that great."

He tried not to concentrate on the fact that Castor's hand was still on his knee.

It was ... a challenge.

Jaffa's nerves were tight. It wasn't the stealing. He'd done enough of that in his lifetime to only have the vaguest of fears on the low burner about being caught. It was Cloud Level. He didn't know what to expect in the most gilded upper crust section of the city. He didn't know how to act.

"We're going to stop off at our place first," Pollux said. "I need to get a few things and you need to relax. Everything about you says uncomfortable and we can't have that if we're slipping in somewhere."

Jaffa hadn't realized how much his pulse was racing until Pollux said that, but he concentrated on unclenching his hands.

Castor squeezed his knee again. Like that would help.

"It'll be fine. I promise."

Jaffa took a few deep breaths as they pulled the transport into the warehouse where they usually stored it. They all hopped out and dragged a wrinkled, stained tarp over the vehicle. Then Castor put a hand on Jaffa's lower back and led him to the door.

"We're going to take the Dragon lifts. There's no point in hiding if we go to our place."

Jaffa had never been in one of the fancy private lifts anymore than he'd been in Cloud City. It didn't make him feel any safer.

They strode through bottom city to the Dragon lift as quickly and confidently as only Dragon lords could. The doors weren't pitted and rusty like most of the public lifts were, and when Pollux touched the keypad with his thumb the doors slid open, quiet and mannerly.

Jaffa hadn't realized there would be cushioned benches in the lift, or that it would be quiet and smell like velvet and a faint pleasant perfume rather than alcohol and a bit too much humanity.

"Jesus," he said quietly.

Castor rolled his eyes. "Come. Sit."

It wasn't a short journey to Cloud City from the bottom. They were mostly quiet but Castor and Pollux shared a few comments here and there.

"What was it, like two months ago that we were on this

lift with Lynx?" Pollux said a minute or so into their journey.

Castor chuckled. "That's the night he met Orion. He was so bumped out."

Jaffa knew what that meant at least. "Lynx? He doesn't seem the type."

"He so isn't. That was a first, and probably a last. But Pol and I were just trying to get him to loosen up. Didn't know he'd up and join the resistance." He snorted. "Glad he did though."

"Me too," Jaffa whispered.

Who knows where his life would be in the next few months, but he felt more stable living in an old office block in the middle of darkness than he'd ever felt in town.

Castor ruffled his hair. It was getting to be a habit.

"Another minute or so," Pollux said. He stood and straightened his clothes.

Jaffa had calmed down a bit in the lift, but his heart started pounding like it had been back at the transport.

"Babe, you'll be fine. If anyone stops to talk to us, just let me or Pol do the talking."

Babe?

Jaffa didn't say anything. He simply nodded.

Cloud City was in a word... spectacular. Jaffa knew it would be but even his imagination and the few holofilms he'd seen around town didn't do it justice.

"I can't believe people actually live up here," he breathed.

It was daylight in cloud city, much like it was in metrolevel and everywhere other than Bottom City and the ruins, but somehow the light seemed lighter, more real. Perfect. The sky inside the glass was blue and gorgeous, the air a temperate warm, and it smelled lovely, like flowers and greenery and sweet baking food. The town square was neat, filled with planters, and benches, a lovely fountain and the odd, mountainous art piece that had started the mess they were trying to fix.

Jaffa tried not to stare at everything.

"It's really not that great," Castor said. He put a hand on Jaffa's lower back to guide him. "Let's go this way."

Cloud level wasn't the giant sprawl that the metro levels had become over the years, so it didn't take them all that long to pass through various neatly manicured paths to the building where Castor and Pollux lived.

It looked like it was mostly windows from the outside, with vast views over the neat expanse of Cloud city.

Pollux punched in a code, then put his thumb in a reader. The main doors swished open and they walked through to an opulent, airy lobby.

"Welcome," Castor said expansively. He chuckled.

"This is insane," Jaffa whispered. The cots at the ruins were the nicest thing he'd ever had to sleep on. He couldn't imagine the existence the twins had grown up in.

They rode an elevator up a few stories, and then when the door opened, they weren't in a hallway but in Castor and Pollux's huge apartment. It was the entire fourth floor. For all they moaned about being insignificant cousins, their place looked like a palace. Jaffa could only wonder what the hell Lynx and Orion's houses looked like.

"Have a seat and try to chill out. Pol and I have a bit of business to do, then we'll head over to the compound and do some digging."

The compound. Apparently Jaffa was going to see where Lynx had grown up after all.

. . .

CASTOR HATED HAVING Jaffa in their apartment.

It wasn't Jaffa, he couldn't think of anything better than being with him nearly all the time, but there was something dirty about their place, about its opulence and its size — especially after everything he'd learned about his family's past.

It was nearly impossible for him not to look beneath the pristine sheen of everything at Cloud Level and not see the suffering that had paid for it. So he hated Jaffa to see it. He wasn't proud of where he'd come from, he wasn't proud of his huge fancy apartment, and he didn't want Jaffa to know that he sort of used to be that person.

"There's a party tonight," Pollux told him. "Gem Arturis is throwing it."

There was always a party. He'd never go to a single one of them again, but that's where he and Pollux made their money.

"Do we both have to be there?" Castor asked.

He'd been hoping to take Jaffa back to the camp and stay there. The thought of trundling all the way back to Cloud City for some vapid social event was nauseating. He supposed they had no choice. He and Pollux had family money, but not nearly enough to be idle socialites.

"I think so, yeah. It would look better if we were up to our usual stuff."

Castor sighed. Fine. "Let's get our arrangements made, then go over to uncle's and get into the storage facility database. I know they've cut off the shipments from the usual hangars, but they have to be distributing somehow. If nothing else, they're storing it somewhere. If we find it, we'll be able to go in and get it."

"Isn't that my job?" Jaffa said from the couch where he was sitting.

"It's *our* job. We're not going to send you in there alone."

He ruffled Jaffa's hair. Again. He also ignored the look that Pollux shot him. Again.

JAFFA TRIED to be calm when Castor and Pollux gave the guards at the entrance of the Dragon complex a casual wave and explained he was a friend of theirs helping with some work.

He'd never seen anything like it. They walked through actual gardens, with ponds and trees and blooming flowers that Jaffa had only seen in pictures. Castor kept a guiding hand on his lower back as they entered through a large glass-front door to a world Jaffa wouldn't have even been able to imagine.

"Lynx lives *here?*" Jaffa whispered. The place was the definition of luxury — rugs, art, soft, velvety furniture — huge windows to let in the artificial sun. It was like heaven.

"Not anymore," Castor whispered back. "And he's a hell of a lot happier now if you ask me."

"Definitely," Pollux said. "Just be chill. We have to get into the business wing. We probably won't run into anyone, but if we do, let us do the talking, obviously."

"Yeah. Of course."

Jaffa followed the cousins through room after room with extravagances beyond anything he'd ever imagined. It seemed like they'd been walking forever before they finally went through another set of glass doors and entered an area that looked luxurious still, but far more utilitarian.

"Let's hit Leo's office. He won't be there yet and he never changes his passcode."

They slid into one of the large corner offices with far too

little care, in Jaffa's opinion, and then got to work while he nervously watched the corridors.

According to Castor's cyber-sleuthing, there was a storage unit in Lower Metro that had a new shipment of *Solorigne*, the drug everyone in New Seattle took to counteract the lack of light. They were keeping it away from the usual shipping docks and from Lynx and Orion, but it wasn't exactly under lock and key — at least not lock and key that would be much of a deterrent for someone like Jaffa.

The place probably was guarded, although that wasn't anything Jaffa couldn't handle. He wasn't surprised it was back down in Lower Metro. Figured there wouldn't be anything as pedestrian as a storage area in Cloud City, even one owned by the Dragons or the Phoenixes.

HE, Castor and Pollux slipped out of the Dragon complex and went back to wait in their insanely luxurious apartment until it the city was flush with an artificial sunset. Castor changed from the utilitarian clothes he typically wore out in the ruins to something that screamed highborn Dragon lord. Pollux did the same, although he tended to go for more dark colors and fewer patterns than Castor did.

Jaffa wondered how they were even considered twins. After knowing them for so many weeks, he barely thought they looked alike.

Castor winked at him and nodded. "You ready?"

Ready as I'll ever be.

Jaffa was good. He'd always been good. But there was risk involved every time he stole. There was always a chance he'd end up in shackles.

Castor handed him a swishy bag with a zipped closure.

"This should be enough to grab a decent amount of it. Pol and I are on distraction duty."

Jaffa nodded. Wait for them to distract the guards, slip in, steal the vitamins. No problem.

He followed Castor and Pollux to the public lift that would take them to the Metro Levels. Not the time for the fancy Dragon lift. Not when every trip on there was recorded privately for anyone in Kovalenko security to see. They all put their hoods up and looked down as they walked into the lift. Nothing super suspicious, just hiding their faces from city surveillance.

"You'll be fine," Castor whispered.

"I know."

Jaffa figured Castor was talking to himself as much as anyone else. He reached out in an uncharacteristic gesture and squeezed Castor's fingers.

He tried not to gasp audibly when Castor threaded their fingers together and held on tight.

"You okay?" He whispered when the public lift shuddered to a squeaky stop at the third Lower Metro Level.

Castor nodded. "Just not the criminal activity I'm used to, that's all."

"I got it. Don't worry."

After that, Jaffa disappeared. He followed Castor and Pollux at a distance through streets he'd know with his eyes closed. They took a turn into an area he was less familiar with, but it wasn't long before they stopped in front of a building with a Dragon insignia on it.

Here we go.

Castor and Pollux started talking to the guards. Jaffa didn't know what the distraction was, only that it had to be enough for him to slip in, get to the storage facility, break the security, steal the medication, and slip back out. Bit more complicated than picking pockets at the market, but he could do it.

He waited until the guards were fully involved with Castor and Pollux, laughing even, before he slipped in through the shadows and started looking for the doorway to unit forty-seven.

It took him a minute to find the red painted door, but then he whipped out the electronic lock picker that Orion had given him a few days back and went to work. Like he said, it wasn't his usual type of job, but it was a bit of a thrill to feel useful again. To *be* Jaffa Sharp once more.

He'd just finished with the locks when he heard feet shuffling down the hall.

Shit.

Jaffa scooted into the storage unit and tried to close the door silently. He didn't dare move, while whoever was out in the hall still could potentially hear him, so he stayed very still for long beats until the footsteps moved away.

He heard the feedback of a comm unit, and the guard reporting that his quadrant was clear.

Jaffa made quick work then. He filled his bag with as many units of the medication as he could stuff in there, then he zipped it shut, checked the hallway, and closed the storage closet's door. Then he crept down, back the way he came and out into the darkness of Lower Metro. He sent a vibration to Castor's comm unit as they'd planned and waited in the shadows of the main square until he saw Castor and Pollux come out.

Jaffa looked once again, made sure they were, in fact, alone, then he jogged out there with the heavy bag on his shoulder.

"Here. Let me take that," Pollux said. "If we come across anyone, it's better for us to have it than you."

Jaffa nodded and he followed Castor and Pollux to the public lift once again.

"Any problems?" Castor asked.

Jaffa shook his head. "Nope. It was easy. Everything is locked up, just like I found it. They won't know a thing until they count the boxes."

Pollux grinned and ruffled his hair like Castor usually did. Jaffa wasn't sure, but he thought Castor might have scowled a bit.

"Let's get you back to the compound and then we have to do our day job. Well night job."

"Getting the rich kids of the city high off their asses?" Jaffa said with a smirk.

"Somebody's gotta do it." Castor shrugged. "Might as well be us."

Chapter Seven

"IT'S BEEN WEEKS, and it's not getting any better." Lynx looked up at the sky.

It had already been so dark it was nearly impossible to see any variation, if there was any at all. It was just the typical oily black expanse they'd all known their whole lives. No light, no stars, no anything.

"How can you tell it's not getting better?" Jaffa asked. "I mean, it looks the same to me, but what's it supposed to look like?"

Castor wanted to reach out and ruffle his soft curls. Over the past couple of weeks out in the compound, things had changed with him and Jaffa. What had been hostile and accusatory that first day had turned into an uneasy truce, which had further turned into a tentative but growing friendship—one that Castor already didn't want to live without.

He desperately looked forward to the days when he could escape the tainted luxuries of Cloud City and make his way out to the damp, dark ruins where he was *happy* for a change and not simply doing everything and everyone he came across in some quest to convince himself of that fact.

The only time he enjoyed in the city was combat training. It used to be a chore, but now he and Pollux attacked it with vigor. He never thought he'd have something to fight *for* beyond his corrupt uncle.

But other than that he never wanted to be there. Away from his new ragtag family. The one he'd chosen rather than been born into.

He never wanted to be away from Jaffa.

Jokes aside, they all knew he wasn't really any younger than they were, but even with his precarious past, he had this sweet, innocent quality about him that was only heightened by his halo of unruly waves, peachy fair skin, and those big, sad blue eyes. They all wanted to take care of him, Castor included.

"Once the cloud's gone, the sky should look like it does inside the city," Castor explained. "Light during the day, dark at night, cloudy when it's raining, but not this kind of cloudy. Not the kind where all the light is gone. Just gray."

"Maybe the cloud is thinning, and we can't tell."

Castor did let himself reach out and ruffle Jaffa's hair for being so sweet and hopeful.

It was as soft as it looked, clean and shiny from newly regular cleaning. Surprisingly, still-cautious Jaffa leaned into the touch instead of away from it. Castor caught Lynx watching them with a small smile.

"Maybe," Lynx said. "But at this rate, we'll all be long gone before any real change happens. If it does at all."

Jaffa was silent for a few moments.

"How far does the cloud stretch?" he asked.

It was a good question. Something most of them had probably never thought about. With dangerous borders and hundreds of corrupt mini-governments all over what used to be the United States, most people didn't travel very far. Not like they used to in the books Castor had read when he was a kid. Not without serious risk of being killed or captured.

Lynx had been out a few times, but Castor and his brother never had. He'd never seen the edge of the darkness.

The cloud had to have gotten pretty big, though, Castor thought, since it had been growing ever since before his parents were born.

"I don't know," was all he said.

Lynx and Orion shook their heads and shrugged as well. The problems in New Seattle were big enough that nobody had really considered what might be happening outside the world they knew.

"Wonder if your families know anything about it? Like, they know the machine's broken, right?"

"Yeah."

"So they have to be talking. This could potentially be a huge problem for them. Without the money from the big pharm companies they've built, half the triads in New Seattle will fall. Not just the Dragons and the Phoenixes, but everyone who's aligned themselves with them."

Lynx cocked his head to the side. "You're right, and they have to know that. They'd have to be dealing with it somehow. There's no way they'd just let it fall without even trying to fix it if they could."

"So can't we find a way to listen in? If they're talking about the cloud machine being broken, maybe they're also talking about why the cloud isn't gone yet and what they can do to make sure it never does go away," Jaffa said.

Castor had to admit, Jaffa had a point. He might not have had much education, but he was intelligent and thought of things none of them had considered.

Already, he'd proven himself irreplaceable to their cause. And irreplaceable to Castor as well.

After only a few weeks, Jaffa's smart mouth and big, innocent eyes had clawed their way into Castor's heart. He couldn't imagine his life without him around.

"I feel stupid," Orion muttered. "We've been so focused on setting this place up and staying safe, we haven't been thinking of the next step. I should've been listening in on their communication all along. It's been weeks. Whatever they planned to do might have already been long since discussed."

Everyone nodded in agreement. Orion tended to take everything on himself. It was one of the best parts about him...and one of his greatest weaknesses. Castor hoped he'd let them take some of the burden. Especially now that he had more of them to take it.

"We had a port to get into the Phoenix system, but it got yanked when Orion was found out," Vela said. "Now all we have is access to the city's main servers, and nothing good will ever go through them." She rolled her eyes. "At least not unless someone's even stupider than they usually are."

"You think the Phoenixes are waiting for you two to try and hack in again?" Pollux asked.

"I'm sure they are," Lynx said. "If we do anything, it'll have to be our family this time. I'm sure Orion's father warned mine about what we did, but maybe he doesn't know what to look for."

Castor removed his hand from Jaffa's hair and casually slung his arm around his shoulder. Jaffa started for a moment but then settled back into his touch. More progress.

He didn't know why it was so important to him that Jaffa want his touches. No, strike that. He did know. It had everything to do with those big, haunted eyes and how he'd started looking at everyone with trust in them rather than jaded wariness. The crust of his past had been polished off until all that was left was a clever, beautiful creature whose mouth quirked at Castor's dumb jokes and who cared fiercely for the people he loved. It was impossible not to be fascinated.

"What to look for where?" Castor asked. He scratched gently at Jaffa's shoulder and was gratified when Jaffa shivered a bit and leaned further into Castor's touch.

"We need a way to get into the communication between the Dragons and the Phoenixes, obviously, but we can't remote hack. Not on a system that's as secure as theirs is bound to be. They'll be notified in a heartbeat if we try a blunt-force attack on the encryption codes from a remote location. That's saying we *could* even hack in. It would be better if we try from the inside like last time," Orion said.

"You think Vela can get to it if you have someone on the inside?"

"Well, yeah. But it's obviously way too dangerous for either of us to sneak onto the Dragon complex," Orion said, gesturing at him and Lynx.

"Hmm, I wonder if you know anyone else who might be able to?" Castor raised his eyebrow.

It was his turn, *finally*. He felt like he'd been practically useless since all this began unless driving transports and being a distraction for five minutes counted. He didn't have Orion's leadership skills or Jaffa's quick thieving fingers, Vela's tech skills or Lynx's trustworthy personality. Castor wanted to *do* something already. He wanted to help.

"Castor, that's too dangerous. We can't have you directly going against my dad." There went good old Lynx again, sticking up for everyone's safety but his own.

"Don't be stubborn. Pollux and I are staying in cloud

city, so we *can* still sneak in. We wouldn't even really be sneaking. This is exactly the perfect opportunity to use us. Not a single person connected us to the medication boost Jaffa pulled off so we're golden."

"My dad's not stupid. He's been on to you guys for a long time, I think." Lynx looked off to the side. "Even if I wasn't until recently."

"Cousin, darling, papa Dragon has no idea what we do. Do you know how much Pollux and I have gotten away with under his nose?"

"He knows you deal."

Castor snorted. "Everyone in the city knows we deal. They always have." He tossed a teasing punch at Lynx's arm with his free hand. "Well, except you. That's nothing compared to the rest of it. I can do this," he said, suddenly serious. "I'm just going to need a bit of guidance."

"You want Pollux with you?" Orion asked. Castor glanced across the room to where Pollux was busily cleaning weapons with Seth. Pollux was laughing and happy, happier than Castor had seen him in a long time. He and his brother were so different in so many ways.

"No. Sneaking isn't something he's good at. Let's leave this one to me."

"I still don't like this," Orion said quietly.

Castor clapped him gently on the shoulder. "Time to let someone else be the hero for once."

CASTOR AND POLLUX were about to leave the compound for the night and make their way back to his Cloud Level apartment when he felt a gentle hand on his shoulder. Jaffa. His whole body knew it. Castor motioned for Pollux to go to the transport and turned.

"What's up?" He asked quietly. They could never be sure that they were really alone out there in the semi-wilderness. It was always prudent to be quiet.

"Just worried. You don't think anyone's caught on to you coming and going all the time?"

Jaffa's eyes looked huge in the moonlight. He reached and curled a small hand around Castor's forearm. He'd started touching Castor more recently, sitting next to him when there were lots of choices, turning to share a laugh, even laying his head down on Castor's shoulder for head scratches like a small, sleepy cat.

Castor smiled. "I don't think so." He reached up and cupped Jaffa's face, rubbed his thumb across a cheekbone that was thankfully less stark than it had been a few weeks before. "I'm pretty quiet about leaving Cloud Level, and they've never paid much attention to Pollux and me. As long as we keep going to our training sessions and showing up for the occasional family meal, I think we're fine."

Jaffa nodded. He didn't make a move to turn and go back into the building.

"You okay?" Castor asked.

"I just wish it could be me. I'm better at sneaking into places."

Castor snorted. "Not so good that I didn't catch you. Have you forgotten that already?"

Jaffa laughed. It was a sound they were all becoming more and more familiar with. "No. I'm probably never going to forget that. Embarrassing." He smiled. "But by far the best thing that's ever happened to me."

Castor pulled Jaffa into a spontaneous hug, the first he'd ever given him. Jaffa felt slight in his arms, delicate and breakable, soft and warm. Castor wanted to protect him so badly.

"Best thing that ever happened to me too," he whispered.

"Because you found Lynx?" Jaffa asked against Castor's chest.

"No. Because I found you."

"I SERIOUSLY DON'T like this, Cas." Lynx's voice came loud and clear through the coms that Vela had rigged. Maybe a bit too loud.

"You don't have to shout. And believe me, after the five hundredth time, I *know* that you and Rion don't like this. It's gonna be fine," Castor assured him. "They're catching a Dragon in the Dragon compound. I even have a level-three security-access card that's all my own to flash around. All we did was soup it up a bit."

Vela had taken Castor's level-three card and made it a black-level card. She'd even coded Leo Kovalenko's access information onto it in case anyone happened to be looking at the server-room's logs. Should be pretty much foolproof.

"Still," Lynx said. "Be careful."

"I will. Is Vela on?"

"Yep, I'm here," she said. "Are you in the server room yet? We're going to have to go fast. I have these coms wired to an isolated circuit, but if we take too long, the Dragons will eventually pick up some chatter if we're still in range of their frequencies. We don't want to raise any red flags."

Castor slipped around the corner toward the main server room. "Nearly there." He could only hope that the Dragons had everything in the main servers and didn't have some super secret room like the Phoenixes did. If so, they were screwed.

"Okay, when you're in, let me know."

"Got it."

He pulled his card out of his pocket and slid it into the reader. "Leo Kovalenko, level five" bleeped on the keycard, and the door hissed open then slid shut behind him, enveloping him in the near-silence of the server room. The only sound was the slight hum of the fans that cooled down looming towers of equipment.

"Vela, you're a genius," Castor murmured.

"I know," she said.

Castor chuckled. He liked her so much. Their individual brands of sarcasm worked perfectly with each other. Most of the time she treated him like an annoying brother, but seeing as though that's how he acted toward her, it was probably fair.

"Okay, you're looking for the terminal that we can use to access one of their ports. After that I can backdoor myself into their system, and we can see anything they can see."

Castor chuckled at the word 'backdoor.'

"You're such a child," Vela grumbled.

"Guilty," he muttered with a grin.

Castor looked around the room, but he didn't see anything labeled TERMINAL. Which would've probably been ridiculous, since everyone probably knew exactly where the terminals were. Unless they happened to be him. Tech systems weren't Castor's strong point.

"What's a terminal look like?" he asked quietly.

Castor could've sworn he nearly heard Vela's eye roll. "Normal. Tracker pad, screen, something you can use to type. We're going to use that terminal to gain access to their servers."

Shit. Castor glanced around the room, counting in his head. There was a screen and keyboard set up on every other tower. "Um, Vela, there are lots of them. Not just one."

"Shit," she echoed. "We're gonna have to move fast. Get to the first one. We'll just go down the line."

Castor jogged over to the side of the room and stared at the screen. "What am I supposed to do with it?"

"Turn it on, then set the decryptor I gave you on the top of the terminal's screen. It should be able to unscramble any passcodes."

Castor slipped the slim card out of his pouch and set it on top of the first terminal. Less than a minute and the home screen flipped onto the terminal.

"Okay, I'm going to request control so I can look for an empty port. I need you to grant it, and then move onto the next terminal screen. I can move faster than the decryptor can. Open them all. Hurry."

A request popped up, and Castor granted it. Then he grabbed his little device and moved to terminal two, unlocking the screen and responding to Vela's access request. Through the room, terminals three, four, five, all the way to seven. Only three more and they'd have them all.

"Aw, fuck," Orion swore softly over the coms.

"I don't like 'aw, fuck'." Castor's pulse skyrocketed. "What's up, Rion?"

"I'm looking at their surveillance feed. You gotta get outta there, you're about to have company. Leo is headed down the hall right toward you. He must've somehow noticed that his access code was used."

"I can do it. I only have to open three more. Then I'll slip out."

"*Castor*. Get out now. We have most of them."

Castor was nothing if not stubborn. He wanted to do the job right. Instead of going for the exit, he jogged to the next terminal and flipped it on, waiting for his device to decrypt the passcode before he granted Vela access and moved to the next one.

"One more," he breathed.

He could do it. One at a time, the terminals started shutting down. He only hoped it was Vela doing it and not someone else.

"I got it, Castor. We're done. Get out of there, *now*."

He cracked open the door and checked. The hallway was empty. Whatever Leo had been doing out there, he'd passed by. Castor slipped out the door and shut it behind him.

"I'm out," he whispered, jogging toward a more central hallway in the Dragon complex. "We did it."

He slipped down the hallway and around the corner before he ran right into his big, brawny cousin. Who'd never quite liked him.

Leo sneered. "Castor, this isn't your usual corner of the compound. Shouldn't you be out somewhere, corrupting socialites and feeding their drug habits?"

Castor smiled to hide how much his obnoxious older cousin made him sweat. "Nice to see you too, Leo. You know, I do actually work sometimes. Like now."

"It's nine o'clock at night."

"What are *you* doing here, then?" Castor asked. His palms grew slick with sweat.

"I got notice that someone in this hallway had used a Dragon access code. Thought it was a little odd for this late at night."

"Times must be tough if number-one son has been demoted to night security," Castor said with a smirk.

"Don't bait him," Orion hissed through his com. Castor tried not to react visibly.

"I think it's time for you to go back to wherever you came from. I'm shutting down this wing for the night."

"Couldn't agree more," Castor answered.

He smiled one more time and went around Leo toward the entrance to the business wing of the compound. Every step that pulled him away from his cousin made Castor's chest loosen just a bit.

"Castor, you okay?" Orion asked. His voice was as tight as Castor's chest had been.

"Fine," he muttered. "I'm going to go home, though. Just in case. Don't want to be seen leaving the city."

"Yeah. Got it. See you tomorrow. You did an awesome job."

Once he was out of the main Dragon building, Castor pulled his earpiece out of his ear and dropped it in his pocket. He didn't feel completely comfortable until he made it through the door of his apartment and locked himself in.

"THERE IS FUCK ALL in these messages. I've looked at nearly every single one of them." Castor pushed out of his chair, frustrated. His back hurt, his eyes were tired, and he had zilch.

"Nothing?" Orion frowned. "We risked you going in there, and there's really nothing at all?"

"Well, they are talking about how the hell to rebuild the damn ARC from broken, messed-up pieces that they can't reproduce very quickly. As far as I can tell from the messages, they don't know why the cloud's not clearing, but they're just panicking that it might someday, so they want to rebuild the machine before that happens. At least we can hope they're just as clueless as us."

"So it's basically a race. Either they'll rebuild the ARC before the cloud clears, or we clear the cloud before they have a chance to rebuild. Anyone want to take bets on who's going to win?" Orion asked quietly.

Castor hadn't seen Orion look so down in the entire time since they'd started working together. He couldn't give up. Whether he realized it or not, Orion was the glue for their little group. The rest of them cared, they wanted to do what was best for the city, but none of them were leaders. They needed him. Castor shot a look at Lynx, who nodded.

"Yeah I wanna make a bet. *Us*. We're going to win. We're *going* to take that cloud out," Lynx said.

Good. That's exactly what he needs to hear. Castor smiled.

"And while we're working on that, we're going to do everything in our power to undermine our families at the same time. Someone's gotta keep them on their toes, right?"

Orion cracked a small smile. Everyone knew he liked nothing more than making the triads look like fools. "Right."

"So we keep looking for a way to break the cloud, but while we're at it, we search for opportunities to score on them and mess with their heads, right?"

"Right," Orion said again. He reached out and hooked his hand around the back of Lynx's neck to bring him in for a small, intimate kiss.

Castor was surprised when a hot shock of jealousy slid through him. He wanted what they had. Not with either of them, of course, but he wanted it with one small, stubborn thief who'd managed to worm his way into Castor's heart in record time.

Chapter Eight

"THIS IS LOOKING like it'll be a bit more long-term than we imagined," Orion said with a sigh.

"No kidding." Castor's eyes hurt from scanning through pages and pages of worthless shit.

Every day they checked the Dragon communications. Every day it was more of the same. He'd learned that the Dragons and the Phoenixes were up to about five million tons of illegal and sketchy things. Not exactly news. But there wasn't anything about clearing the cloud other than the fact that they were afraid it could happen.

Maybe they really didn't know how it could be done. Maybe it was impossible altogether.

"What are we going to do?"

"Well, to be honest, clearing the cloud was never the original intent, was it?" Lynx spoke up.

Between him and Orion, he was usually the quieter one, the background support. Everyone looked at him, and he cleared his throat nervously.

"I mean, yeah, it's still really important, but what about the rest of it? What about stealing supplies for the people who can't get them? What about discrediting the triads and getting rid of them? We can still do that stuff, even if the sky hasn't cleared, can't we? I mean, we were going to do it anyway, as something to do until we figured things out. But what if we don't figure things out? Can't we still do *something?*"

Orion reached out and wrapped his hand around the back of Lynx's neck like he always did. Castor felt what was becoming a habitual painful shot of envy. They looked so real and secure and solid. He'd never wanted anything like they had before; it always had seemed like more trouble than it was worth. Not anymore. And sure, they were stuck in the middle of the big huge mess, but he'd never seen Lynx look so content.

Castor couldn't help but glance across the room at Jaffa. Also couldn't help smiling when he saw Jaffa looking back at him. He wanted to go sit next to him. It wasn't often they were separated anymore.

"Of course we're not going to stop helping people. Even if we can get the cloud to clear, things aren't going to be magically okay," Orion said softly.

Even with his gentle voice, there was still a thick band of steel in there. How anyone had *ever* have thought he was some empty-headed, drug-addled, frosted society confection was beyond Castor.

"What about getting rid of the triads altogether?" Pollux asked. "How are we supposed to do that? Even before our families were in charge, the triads have ruled the city for generations. How do we take them all out?"

"I haven't gotten to that point yet," Orion admitted. "It's obvious we need to get rid of them. I'm just not sure how."

"We can't just let another one do what the Dragons and the Phoenixes are doing," Jaffa said quietly.

"Exactly."

"Listen," Pollux said. "We have a few things to take care of up on Cloud Level tonight. Are you guys okay for the night?"

Castor didn't want to leave, but Pollux had a point. They had work to do.

"Gotta keep the business running?" Lynx asked with a wry smile.

Castor remembered when Lynx had been outraged and shocked by what he and Pollux did. Joking acceptance was a step in the right direction. He'd changed so much since he'd met Orion. Castor was happy for him.

"For a bit longer," Pollux said. "We pretty much always need operating cash, right?"

"Couldn't hurt," Orion said. "I'll pretend I don't know where it comes from. If you sell to my sister, I'll kill you."

"We'll leave your sister alone. Don't worry," Castor assured him with a laugh.

That was a bit too close for comfort. Of course, he and Pollux were definitely not selling to Cassiopeia. She'd never want it anyway. But he wondered how happy Orion would be to know they'd been in contact with her for weeks. Even better, that her and Pollux had some sort of odd flirtation going on. Castor nearly told him just to watch Pollux squirm. Then he decided to be a nice brother.

"We'll be back tomorrow," Pollux told them, his face open and honest. Castor had no idea how he managed to never look like he was up to something.

Castor felt eyes on him. He looked up to connect gazes with Jaffa.

"Be careful," Jaffa said softly.

His huge blue eyes were worried. He'd already told Castor that it made him nervous when he and Pollux stayed in the city too long. Castor reached out and ruffled his soft brown hair. The hair ruffle turned into more of a touch as his fingers trailed down Jaffa's pale cheeks. He so didn't want to leave the compound. He wanted to stay the night, slide into Jaffa's makeshift bunk beside him, and hold him all night long. Castor hadn't ever wanted that. He'd always been all about fun, not comfort and closeness. Jaffa had changed that. Jaffa had changed everything.

"We'll be fine, kid," he said quietly for old time's sake. He hadn't seen Jaffa as a kid since that very first day.

Jaffa rolled his eyes. "I'm not a kid," he muttered.

Castor smiled and chucked him gently under the chin just so he had the excuse to touch him again. "I know."

THE TRIP back to the city seemed to take forever. Orion and Lynx had let them use the faster of the two rickety old transport vehicles, but even with the brush speeding beneath them, the distance to the city felt like it stretched farther and farther, rather than getting closer. It wasn't that Castor was impatient to go back. Just the opposite. It almost felt like he didn't belong there anymore, like now that he knew just how deep the corruption went, he could barely stomach his family any longer.

Lynx had said it had been the same for him, that he could barely look his parents and his older brother in the eye, knowing what they'd been, if not responsible for start-ing, at least complicit in continuing. Every trip Castor made to the derelict building in the ruins made that place seem more and more like home. Even though it was dark and a bit mildewy, although it lacked the clean, expensive sterility of their apartment on Cloud Level, it felt *real*. It felt like he was living an actual life with people he really cared about.

Nothing in the city felt like that anymore. It probably never had. Instead everything reminded Castor of how many people had died so it could exist. How many people lived below and were deformed and sick, so his family could have servants. How many people in the most privileged parts of town were coasting along in a mind-numbing haze, barely existing. It made him want to throw up.

Pollux parked the transport vehicle by the abandoned church, and they hopped out and covered it with brush. Not too many people came out to the outskirts of Bottom City, so the vehicle was most likely safe as is, but it was always better to be careful. They had a long, tense trek ahead of them through the grungy streets of Bottom City to the lifts. Both brothers had been to the bottom many times. But no matter how many trips anyone made to Bottom City, the danger was the same. Familiarity wasn't any sort of excuse for complacency. Rather, it only made Castor more aware of the dangers.

"What's the plan for tonight?" Pollux asked quietly. He obviously felt the same wariness, the press of darkness, of shadows and the unknown.

"We have to hit the Griffin party. I have that whole bag of bump I can't afford not to unload, and did you have a few grams of *starfire* still to get rid of?" Castor asked.

"Yeah, they're spoken for, though. Antila and her friends messaged me this morning."

"Cash only from that crowd. No credit. Not anymore." They needed to make sure they had money in their hand, not an I owe you from someone with a habit bigger than their bank account.

"Probably a good idea," Pollux said with a wry smile. "Hey, quick question."

"Yeah?"

"What's up with you and our little pickpocket?"

Castor's face went hot in literally one heartbeat. "Jaffa?"

Sound casual. Nothing's going on.

Well, nothing was going on. Yet. That didn't mean Castor hadn't thought it every time Jaffa smiled at him, every time they touched, every time Jaffa snuggled closer to him without appearing to think twice about it. Castor's insides melted.

"Well, I certainly didn't meant the thirteen-year-old girl," Pollux joked.

Castor chuckled. "Nothing. He's adorable, you have to admit it, but look what we're in the middle of." Castor glanced pointedly at his brother. "It's not exactly the time for a fling, you know? Or anything more."

Even if he wanted more. Even if he wanted it all.

"Are you trying to tell me something?"

"I'm trying to tell you that I know you were with Cassiopeia again last night," Castor said. "She's a good person, but remember where she stands and who her family is."

"Yeah. *Orion* is her family."

Castor shook his head. "Not unless she's a part of what he's doing. Until then, she's a Phoenix just like the rest of them."

"Maybe we should give her a choice to be on his side." There was something unsettling in his twin's voice.

Oh, no...

"Pol. What have you done?"

Pollux looked away. It was too dark to see his expression, but Castor knew his brother as well as he knew himself. "If you're going to try to lie to me, don't. Just tell me what you said to her."

"Nothing. I swear. Not really, at least. She's just easy to talk to."

"Let's try not to talk too much. I don't really feel like going to prison." Castor rolled his eyes. "Okay, we'd better be on alert."

They were getting close to the Bottom City market. They had to walk through the crowded hot, narrow market to get to the lift that took them to their part of cloud city. The market was old, one of the icons of times long gone, filled with stalls that used to sell fruits and vegetables, coffee, fish from the bay, and flowers from fields that had long since died from the lack of light.

The only part of the past that still remained was a moldering shell of crumbling, half-painted brick and the dim red glow of antique lights which must've been maintained in some sad attempt at nostalgia. Everything else had degraded until it was unrecognizable to what it once had been. Fruit turned to weapons, vegetables to drugs and women.

You could buy nearly anything you wanted down in the bowels of the city—as long as you had plenty of cash and didn't ask many questions.

"C'mon. We need to get to the south corner."

There was a corroded old brass statue of a pig, covered in black slime, right near the lift they needed to get them to their section of Cloud Level. It was yet another relic of the times long gone. Sometimes Castor wished he could see more than just pictures of what used to be. He wanted to breathe deep and smell the ocean, not the dank, fetid swamp that was left. He hoped for the day when he could turn his face to the sky and feel real, actual sunlight.

There was work to be done before they got to that point. Real work and lots of it.

Castor and Pollux wove through the heat of the market, their eyes sharp and hands on their hips, where there were cords easy to pull if someone was inclined to steal their money. Always best to be careful. Castor and his brother knew better than to be robbed. They reached their lift safely, though, and both breathed long sighs of relief. This lift was private and required a code to open, so it was ready and waiting for the brothers to slip right on.

"I'm always happy when those doors close," Pollux muttered.

"Me too. And to think the ruins are supposed to be more dangerous."

The brothers had never encountered any other people at all in the ruins, let alone someone who would slice them open for what little money they usually carried on their bodies. He was glad for the apparent misconception, though. Kept their identities quiet and their location secure.

The lift sped toward the top of the city. The ride was fairly short on their luxury private lift, only a few minutes, unlike the long, droning ride on a public one, but during it, Castor felt dread pool at the base of his spine. He felt like his family would know where he'd been, what he'd been up to.

They'd never paid much attention to him and his brother before, not if they made it to training class and didn't cause too much trouble of the illegal sort. But ever since Lynx had gone missing, Castor felt like Leo was watching them with unhealthy curiosity. Maybe he was imagining it; after all, Leo had far more important things to do than keep an eye on his disreputable, drug-dealing cousins with a MetroLevel mother of questionable breeding, but Castor had seen more of him in the past two weeks than the entire last year. Especially after the night he'd gotten into the server room.

It was disconcerting, to say the least.

"Here we are, home sweet home," he said softly when the lift alighted on Cloud Level.

"Let's get this party over with and get back to the apartment. We have a lot to get done before we go back to the ruins tomorrow."

The doors opened right outside the main Dragon complex into the ornate square where Castor and Pollux's apartment lay. Castor nearly jumped when Leo and his girlfriend Aquila stood right outside the open doors, as if Leo had known they were coming and was lying in wait.

"Leo!"

"Evening, cousin." He looked at the monitor. "I see you two were down in Bottom City again."

"And I see you're watching us...again." Castor tried to look annoyed and not scared. Truthfully he was both. He didn't know where Leo stood, but he doubted it was on the side of Katana. Best not to show any of his hand, including his nerves.

"What were you two doing?"

"We had business matters down below. We're just returning for the evening."

"I know all about your business matters," Leo growled. "Father doesn't approve. I don't either."

"Come off it, Leo. You're not a saint, you know."

If everyone was right about Lynx's older brother, he was far from a saint. He was involved with the leaders of the two triads just like their uncle was, into it up to his pretty, kohl-lined eyeballs. Castor tried to keep his disgust off his face. Instead, he walked around Leo and Aquila. If he waited for Leo to move, they might be standing there all night.

"It was lovely to see you again, cousin. We've run into each other a lot these past weeks, so maybe it'll become a habit. I'll make sure to convey your greetings to my mother," Castor said. He hoped the knives in his voice were sufficiently masked by silk.

"Absolutely. And I will do the same with my mother. Have a good evening, Cas, Pol. Stay safe out there."

Castor wasn't sure if that was a veiled threat or simple politeness. He figured it was safer to assume the first.

The brothers walked about a hundred feet before Pollux hit Castor in the side. "What shit were you pulling back there? Leo's dangerous."

No kidding. "He knows something. I'm trying to figure out what. He's been keeping track of us for days, and I think we need to know why."

"And you're going find out by *baiting* him?"

Castor grinned. "Isn't that the best way? Get someone off their guard? Shake 'em a little and see what comes out?"

"You're going to get us into trouble. Even more than we're usually in." Pollux sighed.

"I think we're all going to get in trouble. Sometimes that's the only way to get things done."

THE PARTY WAS EXACTLY LIKE every other party Castor had ever been to. Vapid society girls, loaded children of crooked triad stooges, the same faces, the same clothes, the same drugs. Castor was honestly tired of it all. He and Pollux had been doing the party circuit for two years, following the socialites and the triad kids, trying to make enough money so they didn't have to depend on their bastard of an uncle for a job. Castor didn't want any more of it.

More and more, even when they were apart, Jaffa's small, pointy face popped into his head: his big eyes, the droopy waves of his hair that grew glossier by the day with the food that Orion's camp provided, and his clear pale skin.

Castor thought of Arlis and Binny too. Jaffa treated those girls like family, he looked at them with soft, fond eyes. Castor didn't want to admit how much he liked it when Jaffa looked at him that way too. With fondness. Like he cared. Castor had come to care about their little ragtag threesome far too much.

"Arlis would like that scarf," Pollux whispered.

He pointed at a filmy flowered piece of fabric carelessly draped over the back of a chair. So Maybe Castor wasn't the only one. Pollux had seemed to take a shining to the two girls as well, cuddling them like an older brother and picking out treats to make them smile.

"Pol, I want to get back to them too. Let's just get this over with so we can."

Pollux went in search of Antila and her friends while Castor took his usual throne in the corner of the room and let his customers come to him. It didn't take long for their stash to be gone and their pockets filled with cash. It never did.

Castor signaled Pollux that it was time to go. Their days of staying and joining the party were gone. He was pretty sure he wasn't going to miss them. And if the brothers left with a soft flowered scarf and someone's jingly gold charm bracelet in their pockets to give to two amazing girls who hadn't had many pretty things in their lives... Well, that was that.

They made it all the way into their building, chatting about their haul, and walked the entire way to the lift before they noticed her standing there waiting.

Cassiopeia.

"Shit," Castor swore under his breath.

They didn't have time for her. He didn't know what he could tell her, or should tell her, he just knew that Orion would kill them if his sister was involved in any way. Orion was a good guy. Castor had a hell of a lot of respect for him, but he knew better than to piss him off. They had to get rid of her.

"Gentlemen," she said quietly. "How are you tonight?"

"We're good," Pollux said with a smile. He reached for her outstretched hand and kissed it. Castor did the same, although he was currently crawling out of his skin to get *on* with it and didn't have time to pacify pretty Phoenix princesses.

"I've heard a few rumors today, boys."

"And what are those?"

She looked right at Pollux. "That you didn't just run into Katana down in Bottom City back when you said you did, but that you saw my brother. That you were with him *today.*"

Castor coughed. "We did see Orion. He was fine, but he didn't stop to chat."

"You can't seriously think I'm going to believe that, not after all the times we've talked about finding him."

Castor hadn't ever been granted such a withering look in his life.

"I mean it. He kind of took off when he saw us. Maybe it's the Dragon red hair."

He smiled at Cassiopeia, tried to sell the story. Castor didn't know what had happened to his lying skills in the past month or so. Even he wouldn't have believed himself.

"Yeah. Still don't buy it."

He didn't blame her. "W-what do you mean?"

"I mean, I know you've spoken with him before. Did you talk to him again today?"

"We haven't—" It was then that Castor noticed the guilty look on his brother's face. *She's easy to talk to, is she? Moron.* "Jesus fucking Christ, Pol. Can't you keep it shut for two whole days?" That's how long they'd been on Cloud Level the last time. Apparently it was a bit too long.

Pollux shrugged. "I didn't meant to tell. She just..."

"Has her ways. Thank you, sweet Pollux." Cassiopeia smiled at him and lifted her hand to his cheek. "Now. I'm guessing you know where my brother is hiding out, and I'm also guessing your cousin is with him. Are you going to take me to them, or are you going to spend the night in one of the smellier Phoenix holding cells?"

"We haven't done anything!"

"You sold bump to my cousin Gemini at that party you just left. And you were spotted with some bags of starfire. Starfire's a bit more exotic than bump, isn't it? It's a much harsher punishment for possession if I do recall correctly."

Castor's pulse sped up. "Who says we had any?"

"Everyone. Including the security monitors at the party. Now are we going?"

"It's not safe, princess."

"Good thing I'll have two trained Dragon assassins with me," she said with a serene smile.

"I'm going to kill you, Pol," Castor grumbled.

"Get in line behind Orion, bro. I can't wait to see his face when we show up with his baby sister."

"Are we going?" She asked again.

She's a stubborn one.

"Yes."

Castor had zero desire to spend the night in a cell. Even more, he kind of trusted Cassiopeia no matter what he'd said to Pol earlier. She might have been an entitled brat, but she loved her brother. No matter what, she wasn't going to rat him out. Didn't mean he was looking forward to Orion's face when he saw her standing in their compound.

"Shall we?" Cassiopeia gestured toward the front door to their building.

"We're going to have to make it quick. There shouldn't be any Phoenix guards in this quadrant, but if we happen to run into any, it wouldn't look good, us being with you. They'll assume the worst."

"That's not exactly true." Cassiopeia made a face. "I might have called a few of my brother's guards to make sure things went smoothly."

"Are you out of your goddamned mind? We weren't going to hurt you, but they might kill us."

"Not if we go the back way out of the building."

"We're not going tonight. Not with your guards all around."

Cassiopeia made a bored face. "Then I guess it's off to the holding cells for the two of you."

"You *brat*." Castor seriously would've punched her. Well, maybe. He wanted to.

"Can't she call the guards off?" Pol asked quietly. Sometimes Castor wondered if he'd gotten all the smart genes in the family.

"No, Pol They're still Phoenix guards. If she says we aren't hurting her, they won't believe her. They'll think we have her under duress. We're gonna have to make a run for it unless you'd like to go to jail and explain to uncle how it happened once we get out."

"Not really."

Castor vowed to have a long talk with his brother about

letting girls flirt information out of him. "So then, let's run. And quietly."

They turned and slipped out the other door into an alley filled with service entrances and the metal doors to garbage shoots. It was still cloud city, sill pretty and clean, but it was a tight alley that was not meant for the pampered citizens. Cassiopeia made a face.

"You think this is below your sensibilities, your highness, just wait until we get down to Bottom City market." Castor chuckled. He heard footsteps at the mouth of the alley and held up his hand. "Shh. They're already out there. Follow me."

The unlikely threesome tiptoed through the dark alley and into the sheltered walkway around the main Dragon square. They had one huge open space between them and the Bottom City lift. Castor only hoped they could run faster than Leonias's guards could shoot.

"We're going to try it the nice way, just walking calm and separate, but if this gets out of hand, you're going to have to sprint, Princess. You go first. We'll follow."

"Thanks a lot," she muttered.

"They're your damn guards, and you called them here. At least they won't shoot you."

Cassiopeia lowered her hood so her sapphire hair shone bright in the false moonlight and walked out into the main square. She made it a few seconds before a guard called to her.

"We'll need to take you home, Princess. Your father's orders."

"Of course they called it in to her father," Castor muttered with a dramatic eye roll. "This couldn't be easy. Phoenix guards."

"Time to run," Pollux said. He gestured to Cassiopeia to

follow, and they started sprinting along the covered breezeway that encircled the main square. There were too many columns in the way to get a good shot, plus one Phoenix princess who they'd be killed if they even scratched, but the guards still took a few shots. The guns made no noise, but chunks of stone flew into Castor's face.

That damn lift better be there. They'd be more than screwed if they had to wait for it to return from another trip to a lower level.

He grabbed Cassiopeia's hand and pulled her into the hallway that led to the secure Dragon lift which was thankfully resting right where it belonged. With shaking fingers, Castor punched in the code, and they slid between the thick metal doors.

Shut, shut, shut.

The doors slid shut just as the clomping footsteps of Phoenix guards began to echo down the hallway.

"If that wasn't the stupidest thing anyone's ever done," Castor said, glaring at Cassiopeia. "You could've gotten all three of us killed."

"I didn't know I could trust you to take me to my brother."

"So you thought the solution was to have us shot for being seen with you?"

"I suppose worry clouded my judgment." Cassiopeia shrugged. She didn't seem too overly concerned about getting either of them shot.

Castor decided to rethink his assumptions about her. The girl was ruthless.

Castor supposed that was the closest they'd get to an apology. The guards had seen him and his brother. There was trouble waiting for them when they returned to cloud city. At best, everyone would assume they were trying to sell drugs to perfect Miss Cassiopeia. At worst, they'd be accused of kidnapping her. He trusted her to a point, but that didn't mean she wouldn't sell them out to protect her brother. Castor knew he had some fast thinking and talking to do.

The lift sank with stomach-clenching finality down toward the Bottom City market they'd left only hours before.

"You're going to have to be careful down here. This is a completely different world than the one you came from."

"I'll protect her," Pollux said.

Castor wanted to punch him. "Of course you will."

ONE HARRIED TRIP through Bottom City and a long bumpy ride on the transport vehicle later, Castor and Pollux pulled a very annoyed and somewhat green around the edges Cassiopeia into the complex out in the ruins. Castor imagined that when she'd said for them to take her to her brother, a long flight out into the creepy, dark-stunted trees was not what she'd had in mind.

"Have you taken me out here to kill me?" she'd asked, her voice wry and sharp. They were all still on edge from their slim escape from the Phoenix guards.

"No, just to abduct you." Pollux grinned.

Castor thought he might puke. His brother, his tough sarcastic brother, was wrapped around little miss ninety-pound Phoenix munchkin's finger and for all appearances he *liked* it there. Course he couldn't really talk, seeing as though his first thought every day was to Jaffa's where-abouts. Part of him was glad to be back at the compound, even with Cassiopeia, so he could make sure everyone was safe. And by everyone, he meant Jaffa.

Castor couldn't watch much more of his brother's downfall, though. "This is where your brother's hiding out with our cousin, Lynx. They're not safe up top anymore. Not anywhere in the city, actually."

Cassiopeia gave him a sharp glance but remained silent.

They picked their way across the short span of cracked, slippery pavement toward the unassuming door they'd been using ever since the first time they'd come out to Orion and Lynx's hideout. They cracked the door open and slipped through.

Cassiopeia looked around with her lips pursed in distaste at the curtained-off rooms, the dingy floor, and entire walls of outdated, patched-together computers. Castor for one was glad to see Jaffa, who'd obviously come out to check who'd opened the door. He knew Jaffa had gone out scavenging for parts that evening soon after he and Pollux had left the compound, and Castor always hated when he went out on his own. They exchanged small, shy smiles and a few touches before Castor turned his attention back to Orion's sister.

"What is this place?" she asked.

"You said you wanted us to take you to Orion? He's here."

"My brother is really here? Hiding out in this slime-infested hole?" Her voice rang out, imperious in the quiet.

"Ye—"

"Cassie?" Orion's surprised call came through a closed curtain. He poked his head around the curtain into the main room. He looked shocked and annoyed. To put it lightly.

"Hello, brother dear. It's nice to finally see you again. I've missed you at home." Cassiopeia smiled the serene smile of a little sister who knew she'd gotten right under her brother's skin.

"What the *hell* are you doing here?" Orion growled under his breath. They were way out in the jungle of the ruins, but he still acted like they could be caught at any moment. "This isn't any place for someone like you."

Castor was a bit afraid of Orion in that moment to be honest, but Cassiopeia stared him down like any little sister worth her salt. Lynx also poked his head into the room. He made a startled sound when he saw Cassiopeia.

"I'm here to find *you*, you moron. What were you thinking, disappearing like that?"

"Aries told me to run." Orion looked like he wanted to strangle her. "If I hadn't, our lovely father would've had me killed. They were going to kill Lynx anyway if we hadn't gotten him out of there."

"Kill you?"

"Yes. *Kill*. That's what happens when the heads of the Phoenix clan find out that their only son is actually the thief Katana."

Cassiopeia looked angry. She looked scared. The one thing she didn't look was surprised. "I can't believe they caught you. I didn't think they ever would. You're smarter than the whole group of them put together."

"Wait, you *knew*? You knew what I was doing." Orion choked and grabbed onto the doorframe with his hand.

She chuckled. "I'm smart too, you know. You're not the only one. And maybe we didn't get to spend that much time together, but I know my brother, and I know what you're capable of. It took me a little while to put it all together. But I have known for ages."

"You aren't angry? You don't want to turn me in?"

"Of course not. You're my brother. I'd never do that to

you. Besides, there are thousands of people who need help and medicine, and if you're the only one who can give it to them, why would I stop you?"

Orion and Lynx exchanged glances. Castor, new to their bond, didn't question when they had their silent little conversations. Cassiopeia didn't seem to have that problem.

"All right. There's obviously more. What is it?"

Pollux crowded into her protectively. Castor noticed that she leaned back into him as well. Interesting.

"There's a lot more, actually." Orion looked at the ground

"And let me guess. Everyone in this room knows but me." She looked annoyed by that fact. Of course.

"Yes. But I'll tell you. You might want to sit for this."

SO HE TOLD HER. He told her the entire story about the cloud and the machine and the medicine. Cassiopeia's face fell further by the minute. When Orion was done, she let out a big sigh.

"I don't want to believe it," she murmured. "I don't want to think that father could be that vile."

"And grandfather, Aries, maybe mother. Probably a lot of the Phoenix council."

"Our family isn't exactly innocent either," Lynx added. "The Dragons are in it just as deep as your family."

"And that's what you guys got caught fixing?"

"Trying to fix. We broke the machine, but as you can see, nothing's happening yet. The cloud's not breaking up on its own."

Cassiopeia considered that for a moment. "And you think you can break it?"

"There has to be a way. We've been looking into old

Phoenix and Dragon correspondence, paperwork, schematics. We haven't found anything, but someone somewhere would've had to know."

"And when you do fix it, the cloud will clear and there will be..."

"Daylight. And a lot of chaos probably. A clean sky, but a mess in the city."

It was a reality none of them were ready to think about. That everything they were doing could easily disintegrate when the sky cleared and people behaved like any large crowd of terrified people usually did.

"That's not any better than what we have now. We'd be getting rid of the Dragons and the Phoenixes, and there would be sunlight, which who knows how that's going to affect the people in Bottom City. Also we'd be leaving room at the top for another triad to take over. That would be just as bad, if not maybe worse. At least the current two have balanced each other out with their squabbling. If a single triad took the lead, we'd have a tyrant on our hands."

"We did think of that, amazingly, but none of us know what to do to fix it."

"Of course you don't. You're smart and brave, but planning has never been your strong suit."

"And it's yours?" Orion asked. Castor thought that maybe Orion didn't know his sister as well as she knew him.

"I wouldn't have said that if it wasn't. Planning and scheming is about all you can do if you're locked in a pristine porcelain tower your whole life. I've been taking over the world in my head since prep school."

"Okay then, mastermind. What do we do? How can we stop another triad from gaining power over the city?"

Cassiopeia smiled, sly and excited. "There are a few ways we can play this."

Chapter Nine

<hr>

CASTOR WATCHED as Orion and his sister stared each other down. He almost laughed at how little Cassiopeia backed down. Nobody else ever stood up to Orion like that other than maybe Lynx. And that was different. Every time Lynx pissed off their great and illustrious leader, he just kissed him and it was over. Castor was pretty sure that tactic wouldn't work for the rest of them. Not if they didn't want Lynx to take their heads off, that was.

"What do you mean, play this? Sis, it's not a game." Orion finally said. He shook his head.

She considered that for a few moments. "It is and it isn't."

"But—"

Orion, poor noble Orion, looked outraged. He took everything so seriously. Castor thought he might see where Cassiopeia was going though. Sure, it was serious, more serious than anything any of them had ever been involved with or probably ever would—but it was still strategic, like a big complicated game.

"No, listen. I've spent my whole life sitting and

watching other people take control and do it badly. I have ideas, and I think it's my turn."

Orion looked like he wanted to protest more, but then he slowly nodded. "Go ahead."

"When I said it's a bit of a game, I don't mean *really*. I know there are people's lives at stake, and it's serious. I'm not like father and mother. I know the people outside of Cloud Level are human and important. But it *is* like a game in that we need strategies. Strategies to get rid of the undesirable players and put our desirable player into the right position."

"Desirable player?"

"Yes, you dork. *You.*" She looked smug, like she'd unlocked the secrets of the universe.

"Wait, I think you have the wrong idea. Cassie, I don't *want* to take over the city. I just want to take the triads down, and then go live somewhere quietly with Lynx."

Cassiopeia rolled her eyes. "And what do you think is going to happen when you take down the triads? Everyone's going to hold hands and dance in a circle?"

"I-I doubt it."

"You know the answer to this already. You *said* it already. Chaos. Chaos is what's going to happen, and that's just as bad the triads being in charge. Maybe a lot worse."

"So chaos is bad and the triads are bad, but I don't want to be the freaking king of the universe. What now?"

"We find someone who does." Cassiopeia smiled. "Or rather someone who won't mind leading the people into a fair democratic system. The dictators have been in charge far too long."

"Exactly who do you think that'll be?" Orion glanced around at their ragtag little group.

She took a long deep breath and leveled her brother

with a stare. "I think if we work things the right way, then that someone might have to be me."

Orion's face went bright red.

"Are you insane? Cass, I can't let you publicly oppose our family. You won't be in any better of a position than I am. It's too dangerous."

"Not yet. That's why I said it's a game. There's such a thing in a game as timing, Rion. This will be all about getting the people ready to accept a change, and then making the change happen."

"So undermining the triads and—"

"And making the people fall in love with you. Or fear you. But I think love is always the better way to go. So that when you tell them I can help them organize into a new government that's fair for everyone, they're ready to listen."

"I don't want them to listen to me, though. I just want to help them."

Castor wondered if Orion was deliberately not seeing Cassiopeia's point. Someone did have to take charge for a little while, or else what came after the triads could very well be worse than the triads themselves.

As much as the idea of tiny Cassiopeia in charge was a bit terrifying, there was a big part of him that knew out of all of them, she was the right choice. Orion was too idealistic, Lynx only seemed to want to make Orion happy, he and Pollux, well, the thought of one of them in charge was laughable, and he didn't think any of the rest of them would even consider it.

"They're going to have to listen to someone at least for a little while, or else we'll be back to square one," Jaffa said quietly.

Castor reached over and rubbed between his narrow

shoulders. He knew it was still hard for Jaffa to speak up in front of the others.

"Chaos," Orion repeated.

"Exactly," Cassiopeia confirmed.

"And then after the government is organized?"

"The people will pick who they want to lead them. That's what a real democracy is like, right?"

It had been so long since Seattle, or any part of what used to be the United States, had had a real democracy that it seemed like such a foreign concept. The states and territories had been divided between triads and military regimes, war was constant, and the ideas of fairness and equality were a thing of the long-forgotten past.

Castor figured fairness and equality never *actually* existed, that they were nice ideals that rarely got put into practice, but at least in the past, the words had some meaning. Maybe they would again.

"We're going to have to work on this, but as an idea, it's good. I just don't want things to go back. I don't want triads or dictators or any one ruler to have too much power." Orion looked pensive.

Cassiopeia nodded. "We'll have to make sure that doesn't happen. And the first step? Undermine the triads. All of them. That's how you'll make the people love you."

SO THEY STARTED small and grew. First there was more medicine stolen from Phoenix and Dragon shipments, antibiotics and fresh bottled water from the Griffins.

Castor and Pollux managed to get a shipment of street drugs off of the underworld-dealing Cobras with their contacts. They didn't give those to the people or sell them, even if Jaffa knew Castor was itching to do so. They got rid of them out in the ruins and watched from afar, laughing, as the Cobras seethed and the media reported large-scale losses across all the triads. It was even more than the media reported. He imagined that people had been paid off to make things look better for the triads than they were. The people were starting to notice, and they knew better.

Just taking from the actual triads wasn't enough, though. The corruption in the city went deep. Their little crew decided to spread their wings even further. Food was taken from the most odious merchants who ran the market and given to people in Lower Metro and Bottom City; clothing and fabrics and new shoes free of holes were stolen and redistributed.

The people learned Katana's signals, and word spread. Soon there were more people lined up for help than even they could provide for. So they picked up the pace, trying to even out the wealth and undo some of the damage the upper crust had caused. The price on Katana's head grew by the day.

"What's next, Rion?" Castor asked one night when they were all sitting around, smiling over their latest victory.

"For now? We keep going. The people need our help, and we can provide it. Get rid of the drugs, redistribute the food, help the people get the vitamins they need. Keep trying to figure out how to break the cloud up while we're at it. The word is spreading. I can feel the shift from distrust to admiration. It's, like, in the air or something."

"I can feel it too," Jaffa said quietly.

He'd been afraid the first few times they'd met with the people to give out food. Not with the little Bottom City children; they knew Lynx and Orion, they loved them. But the new crowds had been tough to please at first, wary and angry, looking for real change and not just a handout. That was evolving, though. People were eager to help, and even those who'd gotten handouts were changing. The streets just felt more organized; the people happier. Jaffa didn't know how to explain it.

It was just...better.

"I think we need to do more," Castor said. "Not everyone has heard about the drop-off points. Not everyone can get to them, even if they have. What if we went into the city more? What if we gave it away?"

"You mean, just drop off supplies at people's houses?" Lynx scoffed.

"Yes. That's exactly what I mean. Maybe some of the people are afraid to be caught, but if the food was taken to them, they can't afford not to accept it. Especially down in the lower city. There's so much poverty even in Lower Metro."

Jaffa nodded. His area had been filled with homeless people like him and the girls and others just barely scraping their way out of Bottom City in tiny, dirty apartments. He knew they needed help just as much if not more than the people at the very bottom.

"I say we try it," he said. "I'm quick, so are the girls. We can help more people that way."

Orion nodded. "I'm willing to give it a try."

Lynx grinned. "Well, I know of a certain house that always has amazingly stocked kitchens. I'd say we give them a visit."

Castor crowed out a loud laugh. "Lynx, you're not seriously saying we should steal from your own house, are you?"

Lynx shrugged. "Why not?"

Katana...Villain or Hero?

New Seattle has been rocked by an escalating series of large-scale heists in the past week by the hood who calls himself Katana and his crew. The robber king and his gang, who once only stole small shipments of medication, have moved to stealing food and supplies along with the medicine. But he doesn't sell it. Katana *gives* it away!

Citizens of Lower Seattle who wish to remain anonymous have reported large gifts appearing on their doorsteps, things they may not have been able to pay for in the past. They're calling our thief a hero.

Katana's crew hit again this evening, emptying out the kitchens at the Dragon complex down to the last crumb. No word has come in yet, but we can only assume he means to give it away like he has in the past.

 What do you think, New Seattle? Is Katana an enemy of the city?

Or is he our...*savior?*

"GUYS, IT'S REALLY WORKING!" Orion crowed. Their crew whooped out enthusiastic cheers.

Jaffa still couldn't believe it. He'd never been a part of anything before, other than the precarious little family he'd built with Arliss and Binny. It felt so foreign but so good. Like he'd been waiting his whole life to fit in somewhere, and he'd always figured he never would, but he did, and it was amazing.

"We'll have a lot of work to do in the morning, getting all this food out—"

"Without getting arrested," Vela added sarcastically.

Orion laughed. "Yes. Without getting arrested. But tonight it's about us. You guys were amazing. I'm lucky to know you."

Lynx hooked up an old music player to one of the generators. They separated some of the food that wouldn't last until the next day, and they had a party. A real party—something else Jaffa would've never been able to imagine. He'd never been more than a meal or two away from nothing. The thought of having friends and fun, people who cared where he was or what he did, had been foreign until he met the girls. Now, he had a family.

And Castor.

Castor, who laughed and spun Binny around in the air. Castor, who danced with Arlis and joked with Pollux and Lynx and hugged Orion and Cassiopeia like they'd been his brother and sister for years instead of enemies only a few short months before. Castor, whose pale skin and burnished hair glowed in the light of their lanterns.

He had an aura around him, beautiful and light and growing bigger by the day. Because as much as Jaffa had changed, Castor had changed more. And Jaffa wanted to be near him. Always. Castor swooped over and tugged Jaffa into a hug just as tight as the ones he'd given to his family. Jaffa's whole body shuddered.

He couldn't help it. Not anymore.

They'd been circling closer and closer to each other for weeks. He felt it. He knew Castor felt it too. Hugs and touches had become second nature, smiles and brushes of their fingers part of each day.

Jaffa cupped his hand around Castor's jaw and leaned forward, brushing their lips together in a shy kiss. Castor's lips were soft, softer than he'd expected, warm and plush and solid against his. Jaffa pulled back.

He tried not to smile, but it was impossible. He'd never done anything like that before. Never kissed anyone, yeah, but he'd also never taken that kind of chance either. That part might have been a much bigger deal. He had to admit it felt good.

"I-I didn't know you wanted..." Castor looked a bit speechless, to be honest.

Jaffa's smile grew. "Yeah. Can't help it."

Castor's lips parted in a smile. His pale cheeks turned a lovely shade of pink. "I've wanted to do that for weeks. Since the beginning. I just didn't know if it'd be welcome. I'm glad you wanted me too."

Jaffa slid his hand from Castor's jaw to the soft gingery hairs on his nape. "I definitely wanted you too."

And then he kissed Castor again.

It was obvious when the others noticed. A few lusty catcalls rang out in the room, and Castor chuckled against Jaffa's lips. Jaffa ignored them and pulled Castor in for more kisses. He wasn't ready to finish just yet.

Chapter Ten

IT WAS dark when Jaffa awoke, as it always had been since he'd moved out into the ruins. It was hard to get used to waking and sleeping when there was no artificial dawn to tell him it was time to rise, but he'd take reality over his old life any day. He'd been grateful every moment that he was in the ruins with people who cared for the girls...people who cared for him.

Jaffa still could barely believe the night before had happened. He still felt Castor's kisses and the soft hand cupped around his jaw when they'd said good night. Jaffa hoped it wasn't a one time, heat of the moment sort of thing, where Castor would pretend it never happened. He wanted it to happen again. And again.

He heard a faint rustle in the murky brush outside the compound. Jaffa's pulse picked up, and he squinted, trying to see what was out there. Some little animal, he could handle. Anything else would be a disaster. A shape moved out of the dark and into the cracked and weed-filled lot surrounding their building. Human, and from the size he'd guess male.

Shit.

Jaffa turned and ran for the doors. He needed weapons, backup; he had to warn Orion.

"I'm not going to hurt you," The man called. Jaffa didn't slow for even a second. "I know who you are, and I want to help."

At that he slowed. "Stay where you are. I'm going inside to get my boss."

The man stopped where he was. Jaffa held up his hand and booked it for the door. As soon as he got in, he started to yell.

"Orion! Lynx! There's a man outside."

Orion poked a sleepy head out from behind his and Lynx's curtained-off area. "What?"

"There's a man outside. He says he wants to help us."

Orion's eyes grew wide. "The weirdness keeps coming, doesn't it?" He disappeared and came back out of his area with a sweater pulled over his head and his fusion pistol held tight in his hand. "Stay behind me."

Jaffa trailed Orion out to the parking lot, where the man had come closer but not threateningly close.

"I'm not armed," he said. He was close enough that he didn't need to shout.

"That's not very smart," Orion said wryly.

"I'm not here to hurt you. I know who you are and what you're doing. I want to help."

"How am I supposed to trust that you're not working for the triads?"

"I was a professor. Look me up. Jarek Orlov. Civic Policies at SPU. I believe it was your father who had me conscripted into a Bottom City work gang for speaking against his laws. If you're taking him and his like down, I want to help."

"Professor? What exactly can you do?"

"I can cook and clean, for one. I'm guessing a band of triad princes can't do much of that. I'm good with computers. I don't have a lot of combat training, but I've done my share of surviving these past two years. I want this to be over. I'll do whatever you need."

"Jaffa, will you go ask Vela to check his name out?"

Jaffa nodded and turned to jog back to the building. He'd heard a smile in Orion's voice.

"If your story is true, then welcome, Professor Orlov."

MORE CAME AFTER ORLOV. One by one at first, then in groups. Teachers, scientists, city officials, police officers—all men and women who'd been ousted from the city by Orion and Lynx's fathers, all barely surviving out in the wild. Their camp grew from a tiny family of rebels to a small town made of fabric walls and more real community than Jaffa had ever thought was possible.

And then one morning, it all changed again. Another group had come straggling in from the ruins, malnourished and pale and tired. Jaffa thought it was more of the same and turned to fetch Orion and Lynx from inside, when Arlis let out a scream.

"Papa!"

She sprinted, hair flying, toward the group of people. One of the men broke from the small pack and reached for her. His arms clasped around her, and he spun her in a circle.

"Baby, I've been looking for you for so long. Is your sister here?"

Arlis, calm collected Arlis, broke into gulping sobs

against his chest. "Yes, papa. She's inside. She's fine. Where's mama?"

Jaffa had gotten closer to them, within a few feet. He saw the man's face fall. "She didn't make it, pumpkin."

"Where have you been?"

"Out here. I snuck into the city dozens of times to look for you and your sister, but I never found you. I thought you two were dead." He choked. "I thought you were dead..."

"We're not, papa. We're okay, we're okay." She turned, face red and puffy with tears, but smiling. Happy. "Jaffa took care of us. He's been like a brother."

Arlis's dad looked up at Jaffa, who all of a sudden felt very small and useless. Jaffa dipped his chin in a nod and turned toward the compound. He had to find Binny. She'd want to see her father. It was the best thing he could do. He slipped through the main door.

"What's going on?"

Castor must've seen the look on his face, because Castor pulled him into his strong warm arms and brushed a kiss over his forehead. Jaffa was relieved for the comfort, but he had a job to do.

"Arlis and Benny's dad is here. He came in from the ruins."

Castor's eyes flew open. "I thought both of their parents were dead."

"So did we. I guess he's been looking for them." Jaffa's throat felt thick and odd. Like it was hard to breathe or swallow.

Castor looked down at him. "Aw, babe. It's fine. They'll still love you too. It's not like he's going to replace you."

"No, it's fine, that's not it..." but Jaffa couldn't finish the sentence. His throat tightened, and Castor drew him back in to a tight hug. "I have to tell Binny. She doesn't know yet."

"C'mon. Let's go get her."

Binny's reunion with her father was just as tearful and joyous as Arlis's had been. He exclaimed over how big and grown-up they looked and how pretty they'd gotten.

By that point, Orion and Lynx had made it outside to greet the newcomers and check their safety. Jaffa huddled close to Castor, watching his girls' reunion with their father. He felt a little weird and empty, and then he felt selfish for feeling it in the first place.

"I think I need to go back to bed." He knew that would sound weird coming from him. He was typically one of the last to sleep and the first up, always wanting to help out. He supposed he still felt a little bit like he had to prove he belonged.

"Do you want me to come lie down with you?" Castor asked. He stroked his hand up and down Jaffa's spine soothingly.

It sounded nice, Castor's solid body curled warm and tight around his, but Jaffa shook his head. Castor loved hearing the stories of the newcomers. The injustices fired him up to keep going to work harder on taking down his family. Jaffa knew that. He didn't want to take that away from him.

"Why don't you go talk to the people who just got here? Lynx and Orion might need your help."

"You sure?" Castor looked torn.

Jaffa nodded. He'd be better if he just had some time alone. That's all it would take to stop feeling weird about the whole thing.

"WE'RE GOING to get all of you settled, but we need to talk to you first," Castor said to the five people huddled around the table in what had become their interview room —two men and three women. They all looked sad and washed out, like their skin had lost the will to be fresh and alive. Arlis and Binny huddled on the floor next to their father. They'd refused to leave his side. Castor couldn't fault them. "I need to know what happened, why you ended up out in the ruins. Who you were in the city."

One by one they told their stories. It was more of the usual. Too much knowledge, too vocal, caught in the wrong place at the wrong time.

Jordan, the girls' father, haltingly confessed that he'd worked in the city office and had inadvertently come across information leading to the existence of the ARC. The Phoenixes had planned to kill him and his family. He'd tried to get all four of them out of the city, but they'd gotten separated, and he'd seen his wife shot down. He nearly started crying when he'd said that he'd not known his daughters were even alive until just an hour before, but he'd never stopped looking for them.

"We'll need to check your identities. It's not a safe business we're in out here, and we need the compound to remain as secure as possible. Soon, though, if everything checks out, you'll be all settled in."

"You don't have to check him out," Binny protested. "He's our father."

"Bin," Arlis muttered. "Let Castor do his job. Papa's not going anywhere."

LATER, after the new arrivals had been admitted and gotten to work finding places to sleep, Castor went out in search of Jaffa. He knew where Jaffa had been sleeping the past few days, in a little closet of an office off the main cafeteria. The room wasn't exactly luxurious, but to someone who'd spent most of his life on the street at worst, or in a tiny abandoned shop at best, it had to be pretty nice to finally have a space all his own.

He tapped on the door frame. "Hey, Jaffa, you okay?"

Jaffa lifted his head sleepily from his pile of blankets on the floor. "I guess. Just feel a little weird."

Castor's heart wrenched. He walked over and bent down until he was on the floor. He scooted under Jaffa's blankets and ignored the hard ground beneath him. He vowed to help Jaffa find something soft to sleep on soon.

"Come here," he muttered and pulled Jaffa into his arms.

His body was still small and wiry, but he had some meat around his ribs finally, and his frame fit perfectly into Castor's arms. It felt like they'd been sleeping together for years.

"I know it feels like you've been their dad all this time. It has to be hard."

Castor couldn't imagine how it would feel. He'd never really been in charge of anyone other than himself, Pollux, and maybe Lynx before Orion took over. He thought of that odd little empty feeling he'd had when he'd realized that Lynx had a new little family with Orion. He thought what Jaffa was feeling had to be about a million times stronger.

"I'm happy for them. I just feel kind of useless now."

Castor rubbed his nose into Jaffa's neck and kissed it. "Not even close. We need you. I need you *so* much."

Jaffa turned in his arms. "You do?"

"Yes. You've made me want so many things, Jaff. Things I would have never thought would be for me."

"Like what?"

Castor cupped his face and brushed a kiss across sweet

pillowy lips. "A real relationship, someone to take care of, someone who worries about me. Love..."

"And you want that stuff with me?" Jaffa's eyes went wide and wondering.

"Yeah, I've been wanting it for a while. I can't even describe how you make me feel."

Jaffa leaned forward and kissed him. "You don't have to. I think I know."

Castor pulled him in for another kiss, this one long and deep, far deeper than any kiss he and Jaffa had shared the night before. He poured everything he was feeling into the kiss, his feelings and his hopes, the way he wanted to spend every moment with one stubborn, mouthy, adorable thief. They kissed and kissed. Castor's hands roamed up and down Jaffa's back. Jaffa panted into his mouth when they gave each other a moment to breathe.

"I had no idea," Jaffa whispered, when they'd pulled away from each other long minutes later. "I didn't know kissing was like that."

Castor felt a stab in his gut.

"I didn't either," he muttered and pulled Jaffa back in for a tight hug.

"I HAVE A PLAN," Cassiopeia said one morning a few days later during one of their quiet times. They were sitting around a makeshift table, eating breakfast from vacuum-sealed cans.

"What's up, Cassie?" Castor had no idea how she managed to sneak out as much as she did.

Even he had a hard time getting out of cloud city sometimes ever since Katana's activity had escalated. The damn

Phoenix guards watched him and Pollux day and night, and Leo's eye had grown more watchful by the hour. Still, he and Pollux weren't guarded like the crown jewel of the Phoenix triad was. Castor had to give her credit for being slippery.

"We need to get my trust fund out of the city. Or at least out of my name. Things are going to be a mess very soon, and it would be nice if we had some money to operate with. Plus, I'm not sure how safe the triad holdings will be at all. That money could easily disappear altogether once we take them down."

"Or be practically worthless," Castor added. Once the triads fell, their economy could do the same.

Cassiopeia sighed. "I can't get to that point yet. For now, I need to get the cash out so it's not held up in Phoenix-run banks. Then I'll deal with the rest."

"How do you want to do that?" Orion asked. "Wouldn't Mom and Dad be awfully suspicious of you starting to withdraw big chunks of cash? If nothing else, they've seen you with Castor and Pollux enough times lately that they'd end up sticking you in rehab."

"What if I hired a new assistant?" She smiled. "Maybe that assistant would be doing such a good job that I'd have to pay her lots and lots of money."

Orion raised his eyebrow. "That could work. Don't you think mom and dad would notice, though? You've never been an extravagant spender."

"No. I'd tell them I hired someone, I'll pay her in cash. That money can come out here and be put away for the time being. Nobody's going to notice. They don't care what I do. They never have as long as I behave." She rolled her eyes. "I might invest in some real estate while I'm at it."

"We should do it too," Castor said to Pollux. "Both of us

have funds tied up with the Dragons that will disappear if everything goes ass up."

"Not that much, just what dad's given us for gifts."

"Not much is better than nothing, Pol. There will be days coming up where we'll need it. I don't think we'll need to be as sly about it. Just start withdrawing small chunks in cash. Make sure our other money is out of cloud city as well."

"Yeah, as remote as the ruins are, they'll be much safer than the city for money and goods for a while if the triads go up in flames. It's going to be a mess there until we can fix it." Cassiopeia nodded at Pollux. "Get anything important out of there. It's for the best."

"How much longer do we still have to pretend to live there?" Pollux asked. "The vibe is getting weirder and weirder. I don't like it. Plus, Leo's up to something. He's always watching us."

"Not much longer," Orion said quietly. "The Dragons and the Phoenixes are holding a benefit in two weeks to aid Bottom City Hospital. I think that'll be your last operation as insiders. Then I pull you out."

"You know the benefit isn't really for the hospitals. Sure, they're going to show some token sum, but they're going to use the bulk of the money to recoup their losses from all we've taken."

Orion smiled. "Yes, I know that."

"So we need to take that money from them."

"Of course we do. And we'll take everything else while we're at it. Their dignity will be ruined, whatever veneer of a good name they have left. It'll be gone. After what I have planned for that benefit, it'll be impossible for you to stay."

"What are you going to do?"

Orion looked at Cassiopeia. She nodded.

"That's going to be the night everyone finds out we're the ones who are really behind Katana. Once we do that, we'll need to be ready. None of you will be able to go back. Cassie, you'll need to be ready to be out as well. Start moving anything you want out here."

"Of course. I'm so ready to be out here." She looked at Pollux.

Castor didn't miss the look between the two of them.

It was real, not a relationship of convenience or because they could sell her something. She cared about Pollux. The way Castor hoped Jaffa cared about him.

Everyone else in his life up until this point had been his friend because he could sell them something or because he was always up for a good time. It hadn't been real. None of them had ever smiled at him with actual warmth in their eyes like Jaffa did, or Orion and the girls, or any of the new stragglers who had wandering into the camp.

He'd never expected to feel so different when they'd first started this. He'd never imagined that he'd actually belong to something other than a family who saw him as a second-class citizen, or a social class that saw him as a means to an end.

He loved it. He just hoped after whatever the hell went down in a few weeks, he'd be able to keep it.

Chapter Eleven

"OKAY, here's the plan. We're going to steal this entire party out from under our families' noses." Orion smirked. "And then we're going to steal the press and tell them exactly what we've been doing."

"Simple as that?" Lynx asked.

"Yep." Orion popped the 'p.' The sound echoed over his coms.

Jaffa grinned. He'd been looking forward to it for days. All the planning and the watching and the waiting—this night was it. He was scared but excited, more excited than he'd been for anything in a long time. He realized Orion had to be terrified, finally coming clean, and in such a public way, but they couldn't move forward until he did.

"Jaffa and Arlis, is your crew ready?"

Jaffa exchanged smiles with Arlis.

Along with her father and a few of the others who'd volunteered to help, they were going to be in place to steal the entire catering order for the party before it even got to the kitchen of the banquet halls. Meats, pastas, breads, and a whole array of expensive simu-fruits and vegetables were being delivered to a rerouted location blocks away from the party, where their team would intercept it and take it back to the compound, where another working crew was ready to divide it into lots and distribute it in the city.

"We're ready." His stomach fluttered with excitement, that thrill he'd always gotten when he was about to close in on a big mark.

"Okay, as soon as you get the food transport, get the hell out of the city. I don't want any of you anywhere near Cloud Level when I make my announcement."

Seth's voice came over the coms. "We need to be at the drop-off point in an hour and a half, Jaffa. It's time to go."

"They're off," Orion said. "That leaves the rest of us. Castor, Cassie, Vela, this is going to be tricky..."

CASTOR TRIED to calm his racing heartbeat as he made his way through the throng of cloud-level citizens toward the donation table. He needed to get there before the main crowd hit the screens. Rather than use coins, the Dragons and the Phoenixes had set up secure direct-donation lines, all funneling into a temporary holding account where it would be divided and sent straight to the Dragon and Phoenix main accounts in the morning.

All Castor had to do was get close enough to the donation station and hit the sequence of buttons Vela had shown him on the cloner he had. It would look like he was making a donation himself; but instead, he'd be hacking into the bank's direct network.

He palmed the device in his pocket and prayed it would work exactly like Vela had said it would.

"Hello, Castor. Enjoying yourself?" Leo. Of course. *Get out of my way. I have things to do.* He had to get to the tables before the rest of the donators. *A little help here...* Just as Leo was about to launch into another—most likely—long-winded speech about how he and Pollux were ruining the Dragon name, Cassiopeia came up and wound her arm through Leo's elbow.

"I heard you have fantastic plans for the old viaduct." She turned and winked at Castor. "I'd love it if you could explain it to me. All those numbers were a bit confusing."

Free at last.

Castor walked on, hurrying as fast as he could without looking like he was hurrying, to the donation table. His hands shook a bit as he punched in the code that would hop onto the network that the donation screens were using. Then he had to get the device back to Vela so she could work her magic, re-routing the money to a separate account Cassiopeia had set up in the name of the charity.

He moved away as soon as the screen showed that they were successfully into the network. Then he passed the device to Vela, dropping it into the pocket of her waitstaff apron.

"We're in. Donation path is re-routed," she said quietly a few minutes later. "Good to go."

All that was left was to watch—as one after the other, the great citizens of cloud city generously opened their pocketbooks to assuage the guilt they had to be feeling about the people who held their entire world up. Vela watched and reported as the totals in their account piled up, bigger and bigger, until it was more cash than even Castor had ever seen. And then it was done. The donations were in. It was time to get the money out.

"Pol, it's done. Everyone's been to the donation tables," he said quietly. "We're ready for you."

"Got it," Pollux's voice came through the coms. "I'm going into the bank."

Long, desperate minutes passed as they heard Pollux ask to cash the account out.

"Okay," he finally said. "Cassie, it's you. You'll have to click through to approve." They'd routed the main Phoenix banking terminal to Cassie's tablet. She surreptitiously pulled it out of her evening bag and approved the transaction. The locator on her tablet showed her at the function in Cloud Level. Everything looked exactly right.

"Withdrawal's approved," she muttered. "Pollux, the money is yours. Take it and get out of there and back to the camp as quickly as you can."

"Yes, ma'am," he said. Castor heard the grin in his brother's voice. It *was* fun screwing their families. Castor couldn't wait until his bastard of an uncle realized he'd been had.

He signaled to Orion, who took his cue. He started weaving his way through the crowd to one of the tables close to the donation table. Lynx was close behind him, head off to the side, not making eye contact with anyone.

"Here we go," Lynx whispered when they were in place. "Make sure you hit your marks for when it's time to get out of here."

Castor slid into place. It was only then that he noticed a small body pressed close to his in the catering company's waitstaff uniform.

"I'm quite all ri—" Cator broke off. "Jaff, what the *hell* are you doing here?" His heart raced at the thought of how much danger they all were in. One more person to get out safely could spell disaster. "If this all goes to hell, you're caught just as much as the rest of us."

"I left the others out in the ruins after we deposited the food. I couldn't miss this. I wanted to help."

Jaffa crowded closer to Castor. Part of Castor wanted to tell him to get out, get far away where he would be safe, but he couldn't do it. Instead, he found himself comforted by Jaffa's slight but solid presence next to him.

Up front, Orion gestured for the news crews to focus on him.

"Good evening, everyone. I'm Orion Leonias. Thank you for coming, and thank you for all of your generous donations to Bottom City Hospital. I'm sure they'll be put to good use."

He raised a glass of champagne, and the confused socialites did the same. They had to have noticed that the appetizers and mingling had gone far too long, probably heard the bedlam coming from the panicked kitchen staff, but appearances and all that. None of them wanted to look like they didn't have a clue what was going on. Castor knew Orion could use that to his advantage and buy some time to do what he had to do.

"Cheers to you all!"

The audience erupted with genteel cheering and the clinking of glasses. Orion gestured for them all to quiet down again.

"There have been rumors all over the city that I disappeared, that I *died* even." He laughed. "Obviously none of them are true. I've been here all the time. The reason I've been missing is, well, I'm not just Orion Leonias. I'm also Katana." A gasp swept across the room followed by an eruption of mutters. "I saw what my family was doing, what all the triads were doing, and I realized that it was wrong, so I set out to change things. Like tonight. The Dragons and the Phoenixes weren't going to use your money to help Bottom City. They were going to use it to fill their bank vaults. I changed that." Orion turned right to his father and winked. "The hospital thanks you directly for your generosity."

Castor watched as both his uncle and Orion's father visibly panicked. At least one of them seemed to forget he was in a huge crowd of his peers. Leonias whipped out his tablet to check the balance in the main Phoenix account. The outrage on his face when he realized the money wasn't there made Castor's entire life. He nearly laughed out loud.

"Not quite what you expected, is it Dad?" Orion said loudly. He had a huge grin on his face.

Both triad leaders made desperate gestures to their security teams. Guards tried to get closer to Orion, but the press crowded them out. For the moment, at least, he was untouchable.

"I didn't do it alone." Orion looked over at Lynx with an indulgent smile. "I had help. Lynx Kovalenko hasn't been missing either. He's been instrumental in helping us get food and medicine to Bottom City families. His cousins, Castor and Pollux...and my sister, Cassiopeia."

Orion's father lunged for Cassiopeia, but Castor and Pollux were ready. They blocked her and backed up, pulling her toward the hallway where they could take off for the ruins. It was scary with the Phoenix guards bearing down on them, but Castor kept moving. They had to save Cassiopeia. She was the future of their plan. Jaffa helped them block, even when he should've gotten the hell away from the guards. Castor and Pollux, Cassiopeia too, they were public figures and family members. The guards would hesitate to kill them. But Jaffa would be gone in a heartbeat, no questions asked.

"Babe, get out of here," Castor whispered as they pushed and shoved at the crowd. "Now."

"We're not done here," Orion said from the front of the

crowd. "There's a lot of work still left. But if we have the peoples' help, we can save Seattle before it's too late."

Orion waved to the crowed and hopped down from his table into what instantly became chaos. The people at the banquet, the press, the guards. There seemed to be no way out. But he'd been smart. He'd put them right near a group of service entrances to the hall, somewhere that people couldn't squeeze into unless they organized into a single-file line.

"We gotta run, guys. You know the plan." he muttered.

Their group scattered. They all had an individual exit plan. The halls for the twins and Cassiopeia, through the kitchens and the laundry for Orion, down the garbage shaft for Lynx, out into the courtyard, under the fence and scatter to the wind. Everyone went a separate way. The plan was to meet where they'd stored the transports and get away before anyone could see where they'd gone. Jaffa didn't have a plan like the rest of them, but he'd spent his life getting out of tight spots. Castor didn't want to leave before he knew Jaffa was safe. Jaffa turned to an exit and nearly slipped out the door, but a rough arm yanked him back. Castor's heart nearly stopped.

"Not so fast. I'm going to need someone who can tell me where to find my bratty little brother and those stupid cousins of his."

Damn. Leo Kovalenko. Big. Strong. And the worst part —smart.

"Jaffa!" Castor called. His entire body twisted into a painful knot.

Pollux grabbed his arm. "C'mon, Cas. We'll come back for him. Jaffa will be fine."

. . .

CASTOR WANTED TO PUKE.

Jaffa. They had *Jaffa*. He didn't realize until that exact second what it would mean to him if Jaffa disappeared into some work gang and they couldn't find him again. Even worse. If Jaffa died. His belly twisted. He wanted to think it was mostly about the girls, that he'd be sad for them if they lost the person who had become their older brother and mother all in one.

But it wasn't about them. It was about *him*. How he'd miss Jaffa's quick, sarcastic laugh, his mouth, his wit, the way his hair flopped over those ridiculously huge blue eyes. The way he hadn't gotten a chance to kiss Jaffa nearly as many times as he wanted to...

"Hey, Cas. You okay?" Lynx asked.

"Just worried." He didn't mind admitting it. Once he'd said it to himself, he didn't mind telling everyone else.

Lynx smiled knowingly. Castor didn't want to know what was in his eyes. Just figured it was pretty telling.

"We found him. I was just coming over here to let you know. Orion and Seth have him. He's going to be just fine. We pulled it off, Cas. The triads looked like fools tonight. And tomorrow, when we deliver the money to the hospital and all of these supplies to the people, they'll be so happy." His face clouded. "I know hero to the people probably wasn't what you pictured for yourself, but—"

"Lynx," Castor stopped him. "It's fine. You're right. I'd have never pictured myself here, doing all this with you or anyone else. But now? Now I can't picture myself doing anything else. We're changing the future, cousin. Us." Castor chuckled and threw his arm around Lynx's shoulder.

"Hopefully. Or else we'll all end up dead."

Castor shrugged. "Maybe a bit of both."

. . .

CASTOR DISTRACTED HIMSELF WITH BANTER, congratulations, and cleanup as long as he could. The hours stretched, though, until he could barely stay in one place more than a few seconds without going out of his mind. They should've been long back. They had to have run into trouble. That was the only possible explanation. Orion never—

"Look who we found wandering around MetroLevel," Orion said with a grin. He and Seth ushered a sheepish Jaffa into the compound.

"Of course, today had to be the day I ran out of luck," he muttered, blushing. "But I had enough left to give ol' Kovalenko the slip." He grinned at Castor. "Seems to be one of my best talents, losing big-headed Kovalenkos."

"Jaffa!" Arlis and Binny ran for him and wrapped their thin arms around his body.

"I'm fine, girls. Just embarrassed."

"We were *worried*." Binny reached on her tiptoes and kissed his cheek.

"Really, it's okay."

"Castor was worried too," Arlis said with a sly grin. "He kept pacing around, looking at the door."

Jaffa ruffled her hair. "Don't stir up trouble."

Yeah, they were in an impossible situation, it was the worst time in the world to get into a serious relationship, but Castor didn't care anymore. He hadn't cared for a long, long time. His whole heart was in it, tangled up in whatever was growing between them and the short time that night when he'd thought he might lose Jaffa. It was enough to know he never wanted to feel it again. Castor lunged for Jaffa and pulled him into a tight hug.

"I was so fucking worried," he whispered. "No more disappearing like that." He leaned down and dropped a gentle but deliberately possessive kiss on Jaffa's lips. *Mine.* "Okay?"

Jaffa stared at him wide-eyed for a few moments before nodding and squeezing Castor back. "Okay."

THE COMPOUND WAS insane that night, wild with celebration as more and more media stories rolled in. News about the son of the Phoenixes who saw the triad's corruption and the Dragon prince who'd joined him. How they'd helped the people, how they were a modern version of Robin Hood and his band of thieves. The Dragons and the Phoenixes had been exposed, and from what they heard, cloud city was on lockdown. People were horrified, outraged, calling for retribution.

Calling for Katana's help.

"We did it," Castor whispered against Jaffa's neck. "The city is ours. The people love Orion."

Jaffa smiled and leaned back against Castor, silently asking for more kisses. "We did."

He watched his friends laugh and dance and joke, content to be exactly where he was, comfortable in Castor's arms.

"Are you tired?" Castor asked. He tightened his arms around Jaffa and pulled him even closer.

"Not really. Are you?" He turned to look at Castor.

Castor grinned. "I could go to bed."

"Are you tired, though?"

"No."

Oh. *Oh.* He really should've gotten it quicker. Jaffa wasn't used to feeling naive. When he did figure out what Castor had meant, his cheeks went hot, and he squirmed against Castor's chest. Castor leaned in and breathed in his ear.

"C'mon, Jaff. Let's go to bed."

Jaffa nearly tripped getting up, and their silent exit was suddenly anything but. Most of the eyes in the room turned to the corner where he and Castor had been sitting, and he got more than a few sly grins as he led Castor toward the small private room he'd slowly been furnishing as his own.

"Well, that was awkward," Jaffa muttered when they'd retreated to his little chamber. "You think any of them know why we came in here?"

Castor chuckled. "I think they all know, love. It's okay." He flicked a switch on the small generator, and then turned on the heating unit and a dim lamp.

The room had been just a simple square with old, faded white walls and polished concrete flooring, but Castor had helped Jaffa bring in a lot of things in the past few days— two thick mattresses that he'd stacked in the corner and covered with his pile of comfortable blankets and pillows, a rug, a bookshelf they used to store Jaffa's things and a slowly growing pile of Castor's as well—even a few pictures Jaffa had found in the ruins to decorate the walls.

Jaffa shyly sat on the bed. Castor had spent a few nights in the room with Jaffa already, but they'd either been tired or scared or both after whatever mission they'd pulled. There hadn't been time for, well, anything like that.

"Cas, listen. I haven't...you were..." *Jesus.* Jaffa had always had a quick mouth and had talked himself out of more sticky situations than he could count. This wasn't even sticky. Just awkward for the guy who'd experienced every-thing in his life but romance. What was his problem?

Castor sat next to him and pulled Jaffa's hand into his lap. "Are you trying to tell me this is your first time?"

"You're my first everything," Jaffa said quietly. "I spent most of my life trying to survive. I didn't have the luxury of really living."

"I kinda figured." Castor leaned over and pressed a slow, sweet kiss to his lips. "Are you sure you want this with me, then? I just want to be with you all the time. Always. I've done my experimenting. I don't want it anymore. I'm pretty sure you already know, but...I just want to be with you."

Castor looked nervous. Unsure.

"I don't want to hold you back if you still want to experience all of that with other people, though."

Jaffa shook his head. He couldn't imagine wanting the hugs and the touches and kissing from anyone but Castor. He'd just gotten used to having feelings for someone. The thought of ever having them for someone else didn't appeal to him at all.

"Maybe I'm not like that. I don't feel like I'm missing out. I just wanted you to know that I don't know what I'm doing. You know. Physically."

"You don't need to. That's not what matters tonight."

"What does matter?"

"How I feel about you, how I hope you feel about me. How amazing it's going to feel to finally get to touch you."

JAFFA NODDED. Castor slowly drew Jaffa's tunic over his head. His shoes and pants came next until he was shivering. Castor lifted the blankets.

"Don't want you to freeze to death," he said. "Get under the covers. I'll be right there."

Castor turned and went to the shelf he'd been slowly claiming as his own. He quickly removed his clothes and rooted through the shelf for a moment before he turned and came back to the bed.

"Hi," he said when he slid into bed with Jaffa. He ran a questioning hand down Jaffa's arm and twined their fingers together.

"Hi," Jaffa answered shyly. His face was so sweet and unsure that Castor just wanted to kiss him forever.

"Let me know if you want to stop, okay? We don't have to go any further than you want."

"I'm not going to want to stop, Cas. I want to be with you. Every time we touch, it never feels close enough."

Castor nuzzled into Jaffa's soft little neck and drew Jaffa's leg up to drape over his hip. "I want to be with you too. Come here. Closer."

He drew Jaffa in and shuddered when their bodies met under the blanket. "I just want to touch you for a while. Kiss you too. There's no rush."

Jaffa cupped Castor's face and leaned in for a soft kiss. "Okay," he said against Castor's mouth. "I like your kisses."

There was something about him. Sure, he was awkward and unpracticed, scrawny and a bit rough around the edges, but he fit perfectly against Castor. All of their parts aligned, melted together, shivered into one lovely mass—even that hard little part of Castor's heart that had told him he'd never trust anyone to be more than a bit of fun in bed. He trusted Jaffa more than he could even say, with his body, his feelings, his heart. Jaffa, who ran his fingers down Castor's spine and shivered into the touches. Jaffa, who deepened their kisses and moaned and used his leg to pull Castor's hips even closer.

They started to move their hips, grinding up against each other. It was Jaffa who began it — velvety skin and hard lengths moving, slipping and sliding. Kid stuff, really.

Things Castor had learned with his friends when he was twelve or thirteen, but it had his heart racing and his breath catching in his throat.

Jaffa's quiet moans and the way he gripped Castor's arms with his smaller hands to drag him closer made it feel more real, more perfect.

"You want more?" Castor whispered. He pulled back a little to look at Jaffa's face. Jaffa gulped and nodded. He looked a little nervous but excited too. "Me too. Lie back. Let me show you something."

Jaffa trembled against the pillows, and he reached for Castor, trying to pull him close again. It made Castor's heart thunk happily in his chest when he thought about how much Jaffa wanted him near. He nuzzled him again on the neck, like he knew Jaffa loved, kissed his ear, and whispered, "I think you'll like this."

Castor tried to remember the first time someone had gone down on him, what it felt like, what was going through his mind. It had been so long ago, so many men and women, that he couldn't really remember. But he wanted to give Jaffa the best first experience he could possibly have.

"Your skin is so pretty," he muttered. Jaffa was pale and small. He'd never spent any time in the sun rooms, just had the regular light in the city and only took the vitamins when he could steal them or afford to buy them with stolen cash. But on him, tiny and white was beautiful. Castor couldn't get enough. He ran his fingers up and down Jaffa's torso, through the loose curls and waves that were splashed on his pillow, along the slim thighs, which parted for his touch.

Castor scooted down until his shoulders were between Jaffa's thighs. He kissed each one, his lips smooth against the thin white skin, following the faint blue lines of Jaffa's veins and gliding over the fine hairs. Jaffa shivered.

"Cas," he moaned. "Feels nice."

"This will feel even nicer," Castor answered with a smile. He took Jaffa slowly into his mouth, letting him get used to the feeling, sinking down and surrounding his cock with wet heat. Jaffa gripped the blankets and Castor's hair. Castor hummed out his approval. He gave Jaffa one swirling lick and pulled off.

"You like it?" He asked with a sly grin. He knew what he was good at. Poor, inexperienced Jaffa didn't have a chance.

"Y-yes," Jaffa choked out.

"Good." With that Castor went back to work, licking and sucking and humming his way along. He was happy. Not just turned on, not just into what he was doing, but actually happy in that moment. He reached for Jaffa's hand and twined their fingers together, let Jaffa squeeze to his heart's content. He used all his best tricks, brought Jaffa to the edge time and again, until he was moaning and crying out and gripping Castor's fingers so hard it almost hurt.

Jaffa rolled his hips hard and curled his toes into the blankets. "Cas, wait, stop, yes, I can't, oh *God.*"

Castor had never wanted to laugh and moan at the same time before. He'd never had so much simple fun giving someone pleasure. He pulled back and dove for Jaffa's lips, a huge grin firmly in place. Jaffa kissed him back, breathless and wrecked. His pretty cock was full and wet against his belly. He needed more. Castor decided to give it to him. He pulled away and sat back on his heels.

"What are you doing?" Jaffa asked.

"This will feel a bit different than my mouth," Castor muttered. He reached over and pulled the packet of lubricant from where he'd stashed it. It had been a while since Castor had let anyone inside—he tended to run the show—but he wanted it for Jaffa. He wanted it for himself too. He worked himself open with his fingers, then reached forward and slicked Jaffa up. It was hard to stop touching when Jaffa was so smooth and pretty. On his knees, Castor shuffled up Jaffa's body until he could line Jaffa's cock up with his entrance, and then he sank down, slowly, until Jaffa was completely inside him.

"Oh my God, oh my God," Jaffa chanted. His hands were at Castor's hips, his eyes alternating between being squeezed closed and staring right at Castor's face. A brilliant flush rose up his chest and stained his cheeks.

"You like this too?" Castor asked a bit breathlessly. He felt full and antsy. He wanted more than just pressure. He wanted Jaffa to *move.*

"It's so, Ohhhhh." Jaffa's voice cracked as Castor rolled his hips. "Wait, wait."

"What's the matter?"

"I almost...just hold on for a second."

Castor watched Jaffa take long, calming breaths. Then he reached up with his hand and ran it down Castor's chest until it was wrapped around his straining cock. Jaffa's small hand fit him perfectly. It felt better than Castor's own hand, better than anyone who'd touched him before.

"Okay, go. Just slowly. This is fucking *incredible*," Jaffa whispered.

They moved, slowly, Castor's hips rolling, Jaffa's hand sliding on him, bringing him closer to the edge with every stroke. Jaffa struggled his way into a sitting position. He kissed Castor's neck, his chest, sucked on a nipple. Rolled his hips and pushed deeper.

"Where'd you learn... oh, *fuck.*"

He'd hit the perfect spot. Castor angled his body so it'd happen again and again. He teetered on the edge. "Jaffa, I'm gonna come."

His warning came only moments before the pleasure started to course through him in hard, clenching waves. Castor cried out and gripped Jaffa's shoulders. Jaffa pumped once more before he cried out himself and leaned his forehead against Castor's chest. They stayed like that for long minutes before Castor mustered the energy to move and separated himself from Jaffa.

"That was amazing," he said softly.

"It was," Jaffa agreed. He reached out and skimmed his palm along Castor's sweaty, sticky belly. "You're a mess, though."

Castor barked out a soft laugh. "So are you."

Jaffa looked down at himself. "I guess I am." They smiled at each other for long moments, Castor brushing his hand on Jaffa's face, Jaffa leaning forward for little soft kisses.

"Hey, Cas?"

"Hmm?" His eyes felt heavy and sleepy like they always did when he was worn and sated. He wrapped his arms tighter around Jaffa and nuzzled his face into Jaffa's soft slightly damp curls.

"I want to try it," Jaffa said quietly.

That got Castor to open his eyes. He pulled back slightly. "Try what?"

"What you just did. I want to try that."

"N-now?" Castor rarely lost his cool, but the idea of being inside Jaffa had him groaning.

Jaffa giggled. "Well, maybe in a few minutes, but that was the idea."

Castor lost the ability to even reply.

Chapter Twelve

THE NEXT DAY came dark as it always did out in the ruins, but still somehow full of light. Jaffa woke in his bed, naked, with Castor wound around him. His body was pleasantly sore, and he shuddered when he thought of the reason.

Jaffa cuddled closer to Castor, not quite ready to get up and face the world. He got tired of the world sometimes, less than he ever did but still. It was nice to have a few hidden moments with Castor.

"What time is it?" Castor mumbled.

"Early, I think." Jaffa hadn't checked. If it wasn't early, that meant he had to get up.

"Good," Castor mumbled. He rubbed the pads of his fingers over Jaffa's belly. "I don't want to get up. Think you can fall back to sleep?"

"Probably." Even if he didn't, he was perfectly content where he was.

"How are you feeling?" Castor asked. His hands wandered down Jaffa's thighs before returning back to where they'd been resting.

"Really good. Why?"

"Just checking." Castor kissed the back of his neck, and Jaffa shivered. "We did a lot last night. Thought you might be sore."

"A little." Jaffa arched his back in a stretch. He couldn't not notice that it brought his backside into very close contact with Castor's hardening cock. He wriggled against it, remembering how it had felt inside him. "Feels kinda nice, though." Castor chuckled breathlessly. "What?"

"I just want you again." He smacked Jaffa's hip lightly. "Quit teasing me. It's too soon. We can't."

"*Fiiine.*" Jaffa stilled in Castor's arms and relaxed once again.

"Soon," Castor promised. "Go back to sleep."

"WHAT THE HELL are you doing here?" Lynx pulled out his fusion pistol and aimed it at the newcomer's chest.

The young man put his hands up to show they were empty and edged into the room.

They'd all dragged themselves out of bed only an hour or so ago. It had been a tiring few days of distributing the spoils of the benefit heist to the people in the city. The more visible members of their crew had tried to stay hidden as much as possible. It left a lot for the rest of them.

Castor knew Jaffa and the girls were exhausted. He had been on edge for days, waiting and watching, hoping every time that Vela or Seth or one of the others left with a small group that they'd all return safely. It was the worst when Jaffa left. He'd wait by the door, nails biting into his palms until the group returned safely and Jaffa was once again in his arms.

Whoever this new guy was, nobody looked pleased to

see him. Castor was ready to show him to the door. Forcefully.

"Rion, tell your boyfriend to put his weapon down," the guy said.

Orion raised an eyebrow and pulled out his own gun. "Not sure I won't shoot you myself. What's this about, Pavo?"

Pavo. Why did that name sound familiar? Castor elbowed Lynx. "Who is this guy?"

"This *guy* is the one who sold us out to Aries. Remember me telling you about him? He nearly got both of us killed."

"That settles it for me." Castor drew a laser blade from his pocket and flicked it on. He wanted to push Jaffa behind him, but he figured Jaffa might object to being protected like that when he could take care of himself.

"I promise. I'm here to help." The traitor raised his hands.

"Like you helped last time?" Lynx asked. "That turned out well."

"No, not like last time. That was stupid. I've been regretting it ever since it happened."

Orion snorted. "You only regret it because my family didn't take you in after you sold me out. If they had, you'd still be there, kissing Aries's ass and feeding him fruit or something."

Nobody made a move to drop their weapons.

"No, listen. I have information your families would want. Information I was going to give to them, but I'm going to give it to you instead."

"Oh yes. Why don't I just believe you and let you in. Everything settled. How'd you find us, anyway?" Orion's grip tightened on his weapon.

"I've been following you for days. You're probably pretty good at dodging your dad's sock-puppet security detail, but I'm a little better than that."

"Fantastic. Forget you ever found us."

Castor imagined they'd be moving soon if Orion's expression was anything to judge by.

"Don't you want to know what I've kept from your families before you kick me out?"

"What you've allegedly kept from them is more like it. *Fine.* Knock yourself out."

Orion made a big show out of looking bored. Castor wanted to get this Pavo guy as far away from their camp as possible. He hoped they didn't have to move. He liked their ragtag home. It was the first place he'd ever felt like he really belonged.

"I know who can break up the cloud," Pavo said. He held up his hand when Orion started to speak. "And I know where you can find him."

"Let me guess. That would be somewhere my family is waiting to take me into custody, hmm?"

"No. It's not like that anymore. Listen, I'll go with you. They threatened me too, didn't they? If your cousin and his stooges are there, I'm in just as much trouble as you are. Besides, he's out here. If for some reason they happened to be there...if there's anywhere you can ditch the Phoenix guards, it would be out in the ruins, right?"

Pavo stepped forward when he was talking, like he had the right to be familiar with Orion.

Orion nodded. Castor wanted to groan at him for trusting the douche. But that was probably what made Orion so much better than him. He was trusting and good, whereas Castor was ready to keep pretty much everyone at arm's length. Except his new family. Them, he trusted implicitly.

"Who is this magical secret keeper?" Lynx spoke for the first time since Pavo walked in the door. He didn't look nearly as inclined to trust him as Orion. He took a step forward, putting his body between the two of them.

Good, cousin. Do what we were trained to do if he makes a single damn move.

Pavo backed up. "He was a professor, a scientist too. Really bigwig in R&D for some huge company. He developed some...*thing*. It didn't quite make sense to me when he told me about it. It's like a bomb with chemicals that can somehow break up the cloud cover in the sky. I don't know about the rest. He had it all laid out. He thought he was doing the city a service, but right before he could present it, your parents took him into custody." Pavo looked at Lynx. "They marched him out to the ruins and left him there to die. He's lucky he didn't."

"If this guy is such a survivor, how did you find him?" Orion asked.

"I'm good at tracking." Pavo shrugged. "You have to remember that. I did it for you all the time."

Orion turned and whispered with Lynx for a moment. Castor didn't miss Pavo's bitter look. Lynx shrugged at the end.

"Fine," Orion said. "We're kind of out of options. Let's go talk to this guy."

"I'm coming with you," Lynx said quickly. Stubbornly.

"So am I," Seth and Vela echoed. Clearly they didn't trust Pavo any more than Lynx did.

Orion sighed. "Listen, guys, why don't the rest of you scatter for a few hours. I don't want you here when I'm not around, now that we've been discovered. The place will be vulnerable, and I still don't trust this one. He could've told my father where we are."

"I didn't," Pavo insisted stubbornly.

"Let's just go. I don't want to deal with you any more than I have to."

The Pavo guy actually looked hurt by that, which made Castor want to laugh out loud. Seriously? The fool was lucky he wasn't dead. He exchanged a look with Pollux. Something in his brother's eyes told Castor that if young Pavo fucked with either Orion or Lynx again, he might not live to see another dawn.

"Castor, Pol, what are you doing?" Orion asked when they went to follow him out the door to their transport.

"Coming with you. There's no way in hell we're just gonna huddle out here in the trees while you're hell knows where with this asshole."

Castor wasn't going to take any other answers, no matter what Orion thought he might say. Surprisingly, he didn't try. He just nodded and gestured for Castor and Pollux to follow them.

"He lives just on the edge of Bottom City," Pavo explained. "My transport only carries one. You can follow me or let me ride on yours."

"If this man is where you say he's going to be, we'll need the seat for him. Take your own vehicle," Orion said shortly. "Don't lose us."

IT WAS A DANGEROUS BUSINESS, riding around out in the unlit ruins—easy to get lost out there in the practically uniform darkness. They'd learned their way around, but there were pockets of uncharted ruin wilderness every-where. If this Pavo guy was angry enough, he'd have no problem leaving them out there somewhere with practically no landmarks to get them home. Castor wished he had a better feeling about the whole thing. He didn't.

They followed Pavo toward the city. That at least was a good sign. They'd have been screwed if he'd taken them further out into the wilderness. He took a sharp turn toward the south section of the ruins a few minutes before they would've reached the old church.

They sped along for another ten minutes or so before Pavo slowed down to a stop. They were parked outside a crumbling brick building perched on the corner of an even older town square. The building looked like it had been a hotel at one point. All that was left now was a sad shell that looked as if it might fall over in a stiff breeze.

"This was one of the oldest parts of the city before it was ruined. I don't know why it's survived as well as it has when the rest of the city has mostly disintegrated. I found him in here. He's waiting for you."

Orion froze. "This guy knows we're coming?"

I smell a trap. Nothing Pavo did made Castor feel inclined to trust him.

"I had to, Rion. He's scared. He's been on the run way longer than you have. Lynx's father tried to have him killed. He's cautious. He heard your names and nearly bolted. I had to tell him the story."

Orion warily climbed out of the cruiser. "I've never killed anyone, Pav. Today might be the day if you've fucked with us in any way."

"What's it going to take for you to trust me?" Pavo asked.

"Nothing. That day isn't going to come."

Pavo took a deep breath and pointed to a darkened doorway. "He's in there."

. . .

THE APARTMENT WAS EMPTY. Just a sad, dirty collection of blackened floorboards and moldering walls. The window was cracked, a small diamond of old glass shattered. There was a mattress on the floor, far newer than the rest of the place, and a few crates piled together to make a makeshift table. Other than that, nothing.

They should've known.

Orion pulled his pistol out and pointed it at Pavo. Castor, Lynx, and Pollux followed suit. Castor, for one, was more than ready to shoot.

"What the hell kind of game are you playing?" Orion asked. His voice was deadly.

Pavo's face flipped into panic. "No, he was here. He really was. He wanted to help."

Orion looked like he was about to shoot when Castor noticed something in the corner. It was another crate, filled with books and blueprints. Sitting on top was a long list of instructions in neat, tight writing held down by a bottle. The pile looked way too neat. Too deliberate. He'd left it for them.

"Orion, stop. Look over there," Castor said.

Orion slowly lowered his weapon. The rest of them didn't. Better to be on the safe side. He walked over to the box and shone a light on it. "I'm pretty sure he left us everything he has. This looks, well, I don't know what the hell it is, but it's a start."

Pollux dropped his weapon and moved over to help Orion lift the box. They carried it down the stairs and into their transport.

PAVO STOOD, waiting next to his own small vehicle. "Listen, I'm going to disappear again. You won't hear from me. I just wanted to do something to make up for what I did. You were my friend, and it was a mistake. I was..." He shook his head.

Jealous, Castor realized. He was jealous.

He'd been in love with Orion, and Orion picked Lynx. Poor guy probably didn't even realize what he'd done to turn his friend away from him. For a moment Castor felt bad until he remembered the asshole almost got his cousin killed.

"It doesn't matter," Pavo continued. "I'll lead you to the edge of Bottom City. You should be fine from there. It's not far."

Orion nodded for Pavo to lead the way out of the square. Castor was glad. At least he was still thinking. If the Phoenix guards were out there waiting in the dark, Pavo would be the first they'd take. He was almost surprised when they weren't. The square was just as dark and creepy as it had been. Silent. Empty. Pavo nodded to Orion and slung his leg over the seat of his transport.

"Glad I could help," he said quietly. Then he revved up his vehicle and sped off into the night.

"That was weird," Lynx whispered.

"Very," Orion said. "C'mon. We need to get out of here. Let's get this stuff back to the compound."

THE REST of them kept watch while Lynx drove. It was hard to see in the dark, even if their eyes had grown used to it after weeks and weeks of life in the ruins. They kept watch as best as they could, though. There were no signs of anyone following. Not even a rustle in the thick brush. Didn't mean Castor wasn't relieved when they got back to camp. Jaffa must've been relieved as well if the way he catapulted himself into Castor's arms as soon as he started crossing the old parking lot meant anything. Jaffa hadn't left like he'd been told to do. He waited there for them. Castor's heart squeezed.

"I'm fine, babe," he murmured into Jaffa's soft hair. "We're all fine."

Chapter Thirteen

"GUYS, I don't know what the hell all this is. It doesn't make any sense." Orion pushed a hand through his long hair, bright sapphire once again, now that the guise of Katana was a thing of the past. "Is there anyone here who can look at it?"

Castor heard the frustration in Orion's voice. To get far enough that they had the answer in their hands and then not be able to do anything about it? Castor himself was frustrated, and he hadn't been involved anywhere near as long as Orion had with the whole thing. Orion had been working against the triads for months, him and Lynx had broken the ARC, and still with the answers right in front of them, they had nothing.

"I can look at it," came a voice from the doorway.

He knew that voice. Everyone quickly turned. Castor took one look at the figure in the door and drew his gun. It was getting quite the workout.

"Leo? What are you doing here?" Lynx's gun was held the highest. He looked like he didn't trust his brother at all. Castor didn't blame him.

"Joining the rebel forces?" Leo cracked a small wry grin. "You guys were awfully hard to find, by the way. I've been looking since the night of the banquet."

Castor and Pollux kept their weapons raised. Lynx slowly lowered his. "You weren't *supposed* to find us."

"Yes, I figured as much."

Castor didn't trust Leo's motives. He'd always been his papa's crown jewel. He had no motive, other than the goodness of his heart, to join them. Maybe Castor was cynical, but Leo's sense of social justice wasn't something he'd be willing to bet all their lives on.

Lynx narrowed his eyes. "Why? Why now? Why not when I first disappeared? You had to have known what was going on. What dad and Leonias were doing."

"Would you believe me if I told you I *didn't* know?" Leo shook his head. "I was aware of some of what our families were doing—withholding drugs from the poor, buying off cops and civil servants, taking care of people who were against them. I spent a lot of time talking myself out of hating it, but I did know—probably quite a bit more than you guys before you started looking into things. All of this, though? The cloud and that machine and how many people our families made disappear for having conflicting ideas? I had no idea how bad it had gotten. It's so wrong."

"I thought you didn't know." Orion raised his eyebrow. "Last time I checked, none of us had told you."

"No, but I remembered Castor being in the server room." He shot an ironic look at Castor. "You used *my* security code to get in. I figured there was something in there. So I looked into it. And I looked some more. That night while dad and Leonias were scrambling to try to get back all the money you'd stolen from the benefit, I was locked up in the computer room, trying to figure out what the hell an ARC was and what it had to do with the darkness. It took me a while to make all the connections."

"And you want to help us get rid of it."

"Of *course* I do."

Leo looked honestly outraged. As much as he thought the guy was a douche wad, Castor had to say he believed he was telling the truth.

Lynx slowly walked over and wrapped his brother in a tight hug. "Then it's good to see you."

"You too, brother. I was worried about you." He glanced at Castor and Pollux. "To be honest, I'd thought these two had done something to you."

Castor made an outraged noise. *The fuck?* "Is that why you've been all over us these past few weeks?"

"Yep. It wasn't out of the realm of possibility that you'd kidnapped him for ransom money."

"It's so fucking out of the realm of *possibility* that I can't even believe you'd think it. You don't know us at all." Castor lunged at Leo.

"Castor," Lynx held him back. "Just let it go." He turned to Leo. "Castor and Pollux were looking for me just like you. They only managed to find me a lot faster. I...I can't believe you're here. What about Lyra?" Their little brother. He was only fifteen. Castor barely knew the kid. He was quiet and sweet and extremely sheltered—hadn't gotten mixed up in the world of parties and drugs and shallow socialites just yet. He didn't deserve what was about to go down.

"I don't know what to do. It's not fair to ask him to leave everything he knows."

"But if what we're trying to do is going to rip the city apart..." Lynx frowned.

"Then yes, we get him out. But let's figure out what we

have to do first." Leo leaned over and looked at the plans. "What do we have here?"

Orion shook his head. "To be honest, I have no idea. I don't know this guy's name—he was pretty deep in hiding—but apparently he was some bigwig scientist who figured out how to break the cloud a few years ago. Obviously the triads couldn't have that, so they tossed him out in the ruins to rot and hopefully get murdered. Supposedly these plans are for a device that he designed that will do it."

Leo scanned over the plans. "I think I can do this." He grinned. "It's been a while since I actually used the big brain I went to school all those years to get."

Lynx elbowed him. "I can't believe you just said that."

"You know I'm smarter than you, squirt." Leo laughed. "But apparently you're quite a bit more sneaky and clever. Maybe you guys can figure out a way to rescue our baby brother."

Castor grinned at Lynx. "On it."

CASTOR AND LYNX crept through the halls of the Dragon compound. Both of them would be apprehended on the spot if they were seen, quite probably killed, but they'd figured that Lyra wouldn't leave with a stranger, and Leo wasn't in any better of a position.

"His bedroom is down that hallway," Lynx said. Castor didn't know Lyra. He'd seen him at family parties and dinners, but like he said, the kid was quiet. He didn't speak much at family functions, and Castor had never really bothered himself to bring Lyra out of his shell. As far as he knew, Lynx hadn't spent a lot of time with the kid either.

"You think he'll come with us?"

Lynx shrugged. "I don't know. But I'm going to do my

best to convince him." He got to the doorway and pulled out the mechanism that Vela had given him to unscramble the door code.

"What makes you think he's even going to be in there?" Castor asked. If it was him in charge, he'd have shipped the kid off weeks before to some corner of the city where nobody went.

"My father wouldn't want to lose control of the last son he has left. He's not going to be gone."

Sure enough, when they descrambled the lock and waited for the door to slide open, behind it was Lynx's little brother, waiting on his bed with a fusion pistol in his hand. He dropped it as soon as he saw his brother's face.

"Lynx!" he called quietly. And then, like a little boy much younger than fifteen, he ran across the room and into Lynx's arms. "I've been so scared. You and Leo disappeared. I thought I was next. Dad's so angry. I've been locked in here all day. He'd have probably had guards on me too, but Dad's always underestimated me, hasn't he?"

Lynx smiled. "He did that to me too. Do you want to come with us? I'm with Leo. Things aren't going to be safe here, and we want you to be out in the ruins with us where it will be. Will you come?"

Lyra didn't hesitate at all. He reached down for a bag he had shoved under his bed and slung it over his shoulder. "I was going to come look for you guys tonight anyway. I'm ready to go."

"Well, that was easy," Castor muttered.

"Hi, Cousin," Lyra said softly. He smiled slyly. He didn't look surprised that Castor was with Lynx. Come to think of it, he hadn't looked surprised about any of it so far. "It's good to see you," Lyra said, his smile growing.

That little shit...

"You know what's going on, don't you? You've known all along."

"Not *all* along. But for a while. Certainly before the benefit." Lyra gestured down the hallway with his head. "We should go. It's not safe for you two here."

"Wait. How did you find out what we were doing? When?"

He shrugged. "A while now. And I'm good with computers. Your hacker is very, very good. But together, her and I could be better."

"How do you know it's a her?"

"Vela? She's a legend." Lyra grinned outright. "I can't wait to meet her."

Castor wondered when he'd stop being surprised by people he'd thought he knew all his life. Probably not any time soon.

They slipped out of the Dragon complex, using Lyra's access cards to get through the doors. He'd be missed, and soon, but hopefully by then, the cloud would be blown and they'd be on their way back to the ruins.

PLANTING WAS THE EASY PART. Of course it was. The hard stuff was everything that would come after the cloud blew apart, and they all knew it. As far as the act of blowing the cloud, they simply needed a place where the city was open to the sky, and that they already had. Right next to the ARC, which still stood dormant and useless right in the middle of Cloud Level, where there was a skylight that opened from a crank in the wall.

"It'll probably blow the hole quite a bit bigger than the skylight's circumference, but the less resistance, the better,"

Leo said. "Just plant it and run. It'll probably shake everything up quite a bit."

"The city's not going to go down, is it?" Jaffa asked. He didn't think they could outrun it if the entire thing were to collapse.

Leo shook his head. "No. Not from the device, at least. People will be able to feel it, though. It'll cause quite a bit of confusion." He looked around the group. "We ready?"

There were six of them: Orion and Lynx, Castor, him, Leo, and their newest arrival, Lyra, who was small and wiry like Jaffa was but with the deep-flaming hair both his brothers had. In less than two weeks, Lyra had managed to become a part of their ragtag little group, helping with small excursions to the lower levels of the city while Leo worked to assemble the device from the blueprints. Of course he managed to worm his way into this excursion as well.

When it came down to it, their little core group had been the most stubborn, apparently, since half the compound had wanted to be the ones to plant the device in cloud city.

"This feels like déjà vu," Lynx murmured.

"Hopefully it'll go a bit smoother than last time," Orion said with a smirk.

"You know," Castor quipped at Lynx. "I'm still not sure that I forgive you for not telling me what you were up to all those weeks. And then when you disappeared, I was half ready to tear the city apart looking for you. You could've sent word, you know."

"This one would kill me." Lynx slung a thumb in Orion's direction. Lynx and Castor chuckled.

Jaffa couldn't believe they were joking. *Joking*, when Orion had what amounted to a bomb strapped to his back in a rucksack.

"Remind me of the plan again?" His voice shook. He couldn't help it.

"Jaffa, watch the entrance to the square. Lyra—stick with him. Lynx, Leo, Castor — You three are my backup. I'm going to set the device up, right next to the ARC. Then I'm going to flip the timer, and all of us are going to get the hell out of there. I doubt we'll make it far before it goes off, but as long as we're not standing right next to it... well, they can blame us, but there isn't any proof, now is there?"

CASTOR ASSUMED they'd get blamed for the disruption. That was until the sun rose and people—hopefully—saw that the sky had cleared, and then they'd probably forget all about the loud noise from the night before. It all depended on the device working. He hoped like hell that the plans had been right and Leo had put everything together correctly.

They snuck into the main square. Orion went right for the center. The other three fanned out around him to keep watch. As Castor turned to check the backside of the ARC, a shadowy figure moved into sight.

"Orion!" Castor shouted.

"Don't even think about it." Leonias held a pistol to Orion's head. "You haven't been my son for months. I won't hesitate to kill you."

"Dad. Stop. You don't want to do this."

"Don't worry. He won't." Castor turned to see Aries Leonias, Orion's cousin, with a laser pistol pointed right at Orion's father. Without even a second thought, he pulled the trigger and Orion's father fell to the ground, shot in the head. Castor gasped.

"Thank you for sav—" Orion started.

"Hand it over."

Aries moved the pistol so it was aimed Orion. He walked up and kicked at Orion's father to make sure he was dead. Not that a shot right in the head left much for chance.

"What?"

Orion looked shocked. Castor couldn't even begin to imagine how it would feel if Lynx had a weapon pointed at his head, so he could sympathize. It had to hurt. First his father, then his cousin. He was glad Orion had them.

"I said hand it over. That thing isn't going off tonight. Just because your father and Kovalenko are finally out of the picture doesn't mean I'm going to hand over the city to your little band of merry thieves."

His uncle was dead? Castor could barely wrap his head around it.

"Aries, you don't want to do this. The triads are done no matter what."

Aries smiled. Castor hadn't had much contact with him, but the bastard looked completely insane. "Of course they are. I shot Kovalenko too about, hmm, an hour ago, and now it's your turn."

Aries gave Orion a chilling wink.

"You really should've stayed out in the ruins, Cousin. I didn't really *want* to kill you. I just needed you out of my way. Now hand over your little device, and I won't make it hurt too bad when I take you down."

Orion whipped out a pistol and aimed it at Aries, who pulled his trigger without hesitation. Castor lunged at him, but Orion was faster. He jumped out of the way of Aries's shot. Castor felt a sharp burn graze his arm.

"Fuck," he hissed. His pistol clattered to the ground.

Lynx stepped out of the shadows. "*Drop* it." He had his own pistol right up against Aries's head, not even an inch between them. "You shoot that thing one more time, and I'll kill my first Phoenix lord."

"I'll kill your pretty boyfriend in a heartbeat."

The rest of them raised their guns to point at Orion's cousin. "And *I* will shoot you before you have a chance," Lynx said. "Put your gun down. It's over for you, just like it is for the rest of them."

The square filled then with police, clomping in with their shields and pistols and night sticks. But they were the actual police, not Leonias's stooges.

"Put your weapons down!" one of them called.

"We'll be happy to as soon as Aries Leonias does," Castor called back.

"Arrest these criminals!" Aries cried at the same time. "They're trying to destroy the city."

"No, we're trying to destroy the cloud that the Phoenix and the Dragon lords have worked to keep. You were involved in that, correct?" Orion turned to the police. "This device will clear the sky. He doesn't want us to deploy it."

The police crowded Orion, but instead of cuffing him, they shielded him as a few officers took Aries and put him in restraints.

"What's the meaning of this? I'm not the criminal. Do you know who I am? They killed my uncle! He's *Katana*."

"Officers, he shot my father. There are multiple witnesses. I believe you'll find that he shot Yuri Kovalenko as well. I don't know where he's stashed the body, though," Orion said.

Two policemen began to drag him away.

"Wait, let me talk to him," Orion said. The police stopped. "What were you doing? Why did you kill my father and Yuri Kovalekno? I thought I could just let them take you away. But I need to know."

"Because they were morons. They were so busy fighting each other and then fighting you that they left the city wide-open, ready for me to take over. Your father didn't even notice when I changed the passcodes to his main accounts and wired the bulk of what was left of his money to a third account that he couldn't access." He looked at Lynx.

"Your father was so busy, mourning the loss of his precious son Leo, that he didn't notice I'd bought off half his guard. They let me right in tonight. That house is mine. The whole thing should've been mine."

"So you wanted the city."

"And the pharmaceutical companies, and the money and the recognition that I've been running Cloud Level for years while your fathers carried out their petty war with each other."

"You could've done it the right way."

Aries rolled his eyes and tugged on his restraints. "I don't want to look at him anymore. Take me out of here."

The police pulled him toward the edge of the main square, in the direction of their Cloud Level holding station.

"Carry on, son," The third said. He tipped his hat at the pack Orion was still carrying.

Their crew silently watched the police and Orion's cousin leave.

"You sorry you didn't shoot him?" Castor asked Orion.

"No. If I had to to keep one of you alive, I would have, but I wouldn't have wanted to."

Lynx reached for his lower back. "It's not who you are."

"Yeah," Orion said quietly. Then he took a deep breath and grinned at the rest of them. "I think it's time to do this."

He took the device out of his pack and set it gingerly on the ground right under the vent in the ceiling where the

ARC had released its polluting gas. Then he set the timer, and they all ran like hell.

Boom.

THE SOUND the entire city to the core. Windows and boulevards cracked, alarms sounded, and for a moment, Jaffa was afraid the entire city would implode, fall in on itself, and grind to dust. Leo said it wouldn't, but there was no certainty, was there? He reached out and braced himself on the wall, watching as little bits and pieces of the building crashed onto the cobbled pavement.

The others looked around too, checking the ceiling above. There was a huge hole blown in it right above the main square, far bigger than the vent had ever been, but other than that, it was shockingly intact. Jaffa was afraid it wouldn't last long, though. The shaking seemed to have subsided, but that didn't mean they were out of danger.

Jaffa saw more armed guards swarm out of the Phoenix complexes doors. Either Orion's father or his cousin Aries must've called for backup before they'd left the complex. He nudged Castor on the arm and pointed. Turned out he didn't need to. The guards started shouting, clomping along the streets, looking for the source of the noise.

"Guys, we have to get out of here. We can't do anything tonight. Not until this calms down a little." Orion gestured toward the lifts. "We need to get to the ruins."

Jaffa was scared. Those lifts couldn't be stable. There was no way. "We should take the stairs," he said.

"It would take us forever to get that far down," Leo protested.

"I know. But I don't trust the lifts right now. What if they've slipped off their tracks? They could kill us."

"I agree with Jaffa," Lynx said. He gave the lift a wary look. "I don't want to put my life in that thing's hands."

"I second that," Castor said. He wound his fingers through Jaffa's and squeezed.

"You guys have a point. We're gonna have to run, though. The nearest stairwell is on the other side of the market."

"So we run. You lead the way?" Orion asked.

"Yeah. Follow me."

Their small group took off through Cloud Level at a brisk jog. People streamed out of their houses in dressing gowns and thin slippers. They looked terrified. Gone was the thin veneer of posh civility and in its place were frightened people, just the same as everyone down below.

There were cries of 'what's happening?' and people shouting that they needed to evacuate to lower levels. They didn't seem to realize that every level would be the same— no safer, no quieter. The sky was rumbling outside the city, loud and angry and terrifying.

Jaffa just wanted to get out of Cloud Level, out of the city altogether, and out into the ruins where he felt safe. He'd never felt safe in the city, but it had only gotten worse when he'd found the place he wanted to call home.

They drew to a stop on the edge of a wide plaza.

"Guys, over there. The Dragon utility staircase is next to that lift. They've never bothered to change the codes. I can still get us in there. It should take us all the way down to Bottom City. We're going to have to get around the people. We don't want a bunch of them following us."

There were already citizens lining up at the lifts, trying to get lower, panicking and milling about.

"Do you think the city will actually fall?" Jaffa asked. He was paranoid, he knew. But he'd never been so scared in his life. He thought he felt the ground shaking. He couldn't be certain. Outside, thunder and lightning made the cloud-level walls flash and tremble.

Orion shook his head. "Leo said the noise would be scary, and it would jar everything, but that it wouldn't actually ruin the structure. We have to trust him. Right now, we have a bunch of scared people, but by tomorrow... Well, the city is the last thing they'll be worried about."

The sun. There would be daylight tomorrow. Real, actual daylight. It would be amazing. And for some, the most terrifying thing they'd ever seen.

"C'mon. We need to go."

Leo keyed a combination into the pad and slid through the doorway into the narrow concrete stairway. The rest of them crowded onto the landing behind him. "We have a long way down. Start jogging."

Down, down they went—the growing chaos from the city echoed outside of the metal doors. People were screaming, and they heard glass breaking. It didn't come from the device anymore, though. It was a riot. A full-scale riot. Jaffa wasn't surprised. They'd been hovering on the edge of one for days, ever since the triads were exposed for just how duplicitous they really were. The people were angry, and now they were scared. It was ripe for disaster.

He tried to concentrate on running, not what would happen in the morning when the sun rose. For a while, he imagined, the people on the inside wouldn't even notice. But word would rise from Bottom City, where the people never saw even artificial light, and soon everyone would know that there was actual light outside.

Jaffa tripped on a stair. His knee wrenched to the side, and a muscle in his calf screamed. Jaffa gasped, and Castor held out his arm

"Are you okay?" he asked. Jaffa nodded, and Castor let his hand slide down Jaffa's arm in a quick caress. "Be careful, okay? We have a while to go still."

Jaffa nodded. His legs were starting to shake. He'd spent most of his life running, but it wasn't the same thing as running down flight after flight of stairs. Still. Better than being stuck in a lift with half of the panicking city.

"We're in lower metro," Orion finally called. "It's not that much further."

Jaffa felt like he'd been in the stairs for a year. The noise outside had quieted. The lower levels of the city hadn't been as affected by the boom. Plus, lower city was typically so noisy that they might have missed the far-off sound altogether, the usual nightly pandemonium drowning it out. They had to have felt it, though.

Finally, the reached another door, thick and metal, at the bottom of the staircase.

"We're here. Follow me. I'm going to lead us to the transports."

Orion cracked the door open and looked around before creeping out. He gestured, and the others followed, walking this time instead of running, blending in with the swarming crowd. Castor snagged Jaffa's hand with his own.

"Don't lose me," he whispered into Jaffa's ear.

They were headed toward the old church, just like on that night that felt like a hundred years ago, the night when he'd led Castor out there, ready to lose him and never look back. Jaffa couldn't believe that he was even the same person he'd been back then. He tightened his grip on Castor's hand and leaned in.

"I won't. Promise."

Castor threw him a quick smile and continued on in silence. They walked, weaving through the throngs of the

Bottom City market, trekked up slippery hills, and finally piled, relieved, into the two transports they had with them. Jaffa laid his head on Castor's shoulder.

"Hey, Jaff..." Castor said quietly.

"Yeah?"

"You were amazing tonight. I'm proud of you."

Jaffa didn't feel like he'd done anything all that special, but still, he was proud of everything they'd accomplished since they'd first began. "You were amazing too. I can't believe it's over."

Castor shook his head. "Nah," he said. "It's not over. It's barely even started."

THEY'D NEARLY MADE it to the bridge that led out across the water, but Jaffa could still hear the chaos from the city. Shot and explosions, bursts of light. He couldn't imagine how terrified the people must be, and how they'd feel in the morning when, if everything had gone to plan, the sun would rise for the first time in anyone's lifetime—at least that he knew. He hoped their plan worked.

Cassiopeia was smart and wily and good, but she was one young girl who was about to be under a lot of pressure. It wouldn't be easy, cleaning up the city. She had some big ideas and lots of people willing to help her. Still, she had to be scared. Jaffa couldn't imagine. He was scared, and he only had responsibility for himself and Castor. Even the girls had their father back. Cassiopeia had a long road ahead of her.

It felt like hours before they reached their safe little camp far from the disaster of the main city. They had a short respite before real chaos would come with the dawn. Time to plan and hope and celebrate what they'd already accomplished, which was already far more than Jaffa had ever thought possible in his small little life.

Castor helped him down from the transport, kissed his forehead, and slid their fingers together. Jaffa's leg hurt, but it didn't matter. He was alive to see a revolution.

THE STARS CAME out that night for the first time in Castor's life, for the first time in their generation, or the one before that. He stood, his arms looped loosely around Jaffa, with his cousins and his closest friends, watching as the clouds slowly drew apart and the sky opened up, sparkling and more beautiful that anything he'd ever seen.

He thought there might be a few tears in the group. Even as cynical as he was and impervious to emotion most of the time, Castor's eyes grew wet and his chest tightened. It was amazing, and something he'd never thought he would see.

"It's beautiful, isn't it?" Jaffa whispered.

"Yeah. I can't believe it's even real." He'd seen pictures of stars, projections, the false sky inside the city, but nothing compared to the vastness of the real heavens. It was awe inspiring.

"I can't even imagine what it's going to be like when the sun comes up."

Amazing, terrifying, probably dangerous as well.

"None of us can. It's going to be hard there for a while. People aren't ready. We tried to spread the word yesterday in the lower city, but I doubt many of them believed us."

"Everything's going to change."

Castor chuckled. That was an understatement, to say the least.

Even with the marvel of the stars, their little ragtag

group of rebels was tired. They'd all had quite a long day, brilliant and sad and scary and exhausting. Eyes began to droop.

"I'll take first watch," Castor volunteered.

He'd never needed as much sleep as the others, and he hadn't had his fill of the sky yet. Apparently none of them had, because everybody dragged blankets and pillows out to the little hill of dirt on the edge of the parking area and spread them out to look at the stars.

Orion nodded and tossed Castor his fusion pistol. "Wake me in an hour. I'll take second watch."

Castor wriggled until he was propped up against the side of a rock, gazing up at the sky with Jaffa's soft curly head in his lap. He ran his fingers through Jaffa's hair, marveling as much at the reality of them as the reality of a whole new world about to dawn on them. Castor wasn't the same person anymore. He barely recognized himself. He barely recognized any of them.

He did sleep when it was his turn, his arms wrapped tightly around Jaffa, their bodies aligned for warmth, and by that point, familiarity. Castor didn't know if he'd ever be able to go back to sleeping without Jaffa. He didn't want to try. He woke when he felt the others shifting around him, murmuring quietly.

"It's almost dawn," Cassiopeia whispered. Sure, they'd all seen hundreds of technically perfect dawns, but none of them wanted to miss this, their first *real* one. They all stood slowly, stretching, and one by one fell silent. It was nearly there. The sky, which had been the most midnight of blackish blues, started to fade to purple, and then blush the most beautiful shade of pink Castor had ever seen.

"It's really happening," he whispered to Jaffa. "It's real."

Jaffa grabbed his hand and laced their fingers tightly

together as they gazed out into the horizon. Pink turned to a pale diaphanous blue, and then it happened. The sun, the real sun, peeked warm and fresh and beautiful over the horizon.

They all grabbed for each other; hugs and hands and kisses and soft shocked cheers went around their little circle.

It was time.

Castor watched as Orion gazed at the sky for one last awestruck moment, then turned to his sister with a smile. "Are you ready?" he asked.

Cassiopeia breathed in, secure in the circle of Pollux's arms, but also strong and deep and true all on her own.

"Is anyone ever really ready?" She asked.

She was right. None of them were ready, and they probably never would be, even when everything they had to do was long over.

"True." Orion shrugged with a grin. "I suppose now is as good of a time as any, though. Okay, everyone. Let's go."

About the Author

MJ O'Shea has never met a music festival, paintbrush, or flower crown she can stay away from. She loves rainstorms and a perfect cup of tea, beach days, music, bright colors, and more than anything a cozy evening with a really great book.

She is from the Pacific Northwest. While she still lives there and loves it, MJ has the heart of a wanderer. So she puts all her dreams of far off places and extraordinary people in her books.

Except for every once in a while when she does what all travelers have to do on occasion … comes home.

www.ingramcontent.com/pod-product-compliance
Lightning Source LLC
Chambersburg PA
CBHW061528120726
48001CB00004B/1439